Acknowledgement

The author wishes to acknowledge the assistance of Mrs. Terri Vilardo and Mr. Larry Berg in proofing and editing an early draft and Mr. Jim Myers and Dr. Michael Bishop for advice in writing this book.

Dedication

Without the love, encouragement, and confidence of my wife Gayle nothing that I accomplished would have been possible. Therefore, this work is dedicated to her with all my love and admiration.

Chapter 1
The Setup

In an Orlando courtroom Judge Bridges looked down on the defendant standing before him. Years of abusing drugs and alcohol made the defendant look older than his 28 years. His unshaven beard, scruffy long hair and rumpled clothes made him look more like a street person than a member of a respectable middle class family.

"Do you understand the consequences of your pleading guilty to the charges and the terms of your probation?"

"Yea" responded the defendant in a silent yet disrespectful tone.

"Let me re-phrase that question. Do you realize that if you abuse alcohol or use, possess or sell illegal drugs you will be sent to the Florida State Penitentiary for a very long time?"

"Yea" once again responded the defendant.

"Boy, let me ask you one more time. Do you understand that if you use, possess or sell illegal drugs or are found operating a motor vehicle impaired or intoxicated in a public place this will be a violation of your probation and you will be sent to the state prison for ten to twenty years? Do you understand these conditions?"

This time before the young man could answer his court appointed public defender whispered something to his client. The attorney had argued cases before Judge Bridges previously and knew him to be a stern, conservative and traditional jurist who had a reputation for rendering the maximum sentence to drug offenders. If he thought the defendant to be disrespectful he would have no qualms in vacating the plea agreement and sending the defendant to prison. The attorney's words to his client were to show maximum respect for the court.

This time the young man looked up at the judge and responded "Yes sir."

"Good, then this matter is ended, court adjourned."

With those words Billie Franklin left the courthouse, got into a waiting white Lexus and rode off.

*****

Meanwhile over a thousand miles away, Jack Victor sat in the library cafeteria finishing his chicken sandwich, small bag of popcorn and a diet Coke. As he looked out the window to the open campus he decided that he would take the long way back to his office. As he exited the building the smell and slight chill of a crisp fall day in this Midwestern college town felt invigorating. He leisurely walked along the tree lined path toward the old quad. The flower beds along the way were in full bloom with red and white mums. The campus was amassed with color in preparation for homecoming weekend. The landscaping crews always seemed to do their best work whenever a large number of alumni were coming to town. One of the landscapers once remarked to Jack that a beautiful campus means a beautiful contribution. The campus felt alive, everyone was talking about the Cougars' football game against State and a possible bowl bid. Signs were hanging in office windows proclaiming "We are the Cougars" and "Beat the Lions". It was a day like this that he was glad to be a college professor. He thought to himself how right he was to turn down the job to work for Health Policy Research Center in Rockville, Maryland six years earlier.

The tranquility was broken by the ringing of his cell phone.

"Jack, Naomi here. Vern just showed me the September financial report and I think we should have

3

an executive committee meeting before the next board meeting. Can you come over around 4:30 today?"

"Yes my afternoon is open. I guess another month of red ink."

"Not good, we'll fill you in when you get here. No use spoiling a beautiful day."

Naomi Hoag was the hospital CEO for the past two years. She had been hired during Jack's first term as Board President. Jack chaired the search and screen committee and while impressed with her credentials she was not his first choice, he preferred the candidate from Wisconsin. But after she had been on the job for a few months, Jack came to respect and appreciate her talents. The Board was looking for an individual who would stand up to the physicians who were gaining more power and influence over the management of the hospital. Their real first success was staging a virtual coup to oust the former popular CEO who served the Hospital for 19 years. Jack thought of her as a tough woman with the tenacity of a shark, she seemed to thrive on controversy and never shied away from a good fight. It was this tenacity, a quality the board sought in the new CEO that put her on the outs with the medical staff. She had a slight dictatorial management style and a hot temper. During her board orientation she told Jack she came to make the hospital money not to make friends.

Jack arrived at the Hospital administration wing a little past four thirty.

"Good afternoon Mr. Victor, the committee's in the board room. Would you like some coffee?"

"No thanks Bonnie."

Sitting around the conference table were Naomi Hoag, Vern Dailey CFO, Geno Peroni COO, Greg Martinelli the board treasurer and the board vice president Pam Summers.

"After lunch Vern showed me the financials for last month. The numbers are not good and that's why I wanted to meet with the executive committee before the full board meeting. Vern you want to share the bad news?"

Vern Dailey gave each member a copy of the previous month's financial report. He went right to the bottom line.

"Another losing month, operating loss for the month was just under $750,000. This makes the seventh month in a row with a net loss. If it were not for the high incidence of flu last January we would have experienced a net loss every month this year. That combined with the virtual zero operating margin last year means we are currently not in very good financial shape. The quarterly payment on the bonds we issued to purchase the new MRI is due next month. Our projections are that unless we see a turn

5

around we will have exhausted our reserve fund by the end of the second quarter of next fiscal year. There is also serious talk that Medicare will once again reduce payments to hospitals in an attempt to reduce an already large federal deficit. Medicare's DRG's now only cover about 75% of the cost of care."

"Thanks Vern." Naomi went on to explain "It seems like once again hospitals will be financing the president's war. Administration has been meeting to develop a strategy to reduce expenses. Since the hospital is labor intensive it looks like some big employee layoffs are in the future. We achieved some attrition with the early retirement incentives the board approved last month, but we have bottomed out on that. It looks like we harvested all the low hanging fruit. Now comes the hard part. We may be able to stop the hemorrhaging; but I hope it's not too late."

After a short pause Jack breaks the silence- "Naomi, I'm glad to hear that administration will be presenting a strategy along with the financial reports. If you don't, I know the board members will be pretty pissed- especially Jefferson he's always ready to rip into us. Wish he'd run the University as well as he thinks he can run a hospital."

The committee continued to focus on trying to find alternatives to staff reductions but the decision kept coming back to employee layoffs as the only viable alternative. After about 75 minutes of discussion

Jack said that the committee would wait for the administration's plan and that there was not much more they could accomplish for now. As the members got up to leave Pam Summers said in jest-

"Maybe we can find someone to buy us before we go broke."

They all laughed.

*****

It was a cold and stark November day, Jack Victor sat at his desk and stared at the pile of papers yet to be graded. Only two more to read and he would have met his goal of ten per day. Grading was the one part of the teaching profession that he disliked the most. Each semester he wrestled with the idea of not requiring a major paper but either for pedagogical reasons, general principles or just to be a hard ass he always included a major paper in the course syllabus. After six years of teaching health policy at the state university you think he would find a better way to grade term papers but no such magic formula was found. Hopefully he would have them all graded before the weekend so he could watch some of the football games. Oh well, yet another paper on the Canadian health care system.

The ringing of the phone interrupted his concentration. "Damn! I forgot to unplug the phone." With some hesitation and a sense of frustration in his voice he reluctantly answered. "Jack", Jennifer announced, "I know you don't want to be interrupted but Ms. Hoag is on the phone and she says it is very important. Do you want me to tell her you'll call her back?"

"No, I'll talk to her."

"Hi Naomi, what's up?"

"I know you are grading papers and didn't want to be interrupted but I think this is important. Are you sitting down?"

"Yes, who's suing us now?"

"No Jack, I don't think it is that simple."

"Not another Stallworth incident?"

"Even, more severe. Rook just left my office. He came by to tell me that he and Rose are preparing papers to tender a formal offer to buy Midland General. From the tone of his voice they are serious and ready to play hard-ball."

"Well, we knew something like this would be coming, I was hoping it would be later rather than sooner like two years from now when my term as board president ended. Naomi what kind of time line do we have? Have you seen the offer? Knowing Rose he probably wanted an answer yesterday."

"No Jack. we have nothing in writing yet, but I agree with you that Rose won't give us much time."

"Well, you made my day. Let me know as soon as you get something from Rook and Rose. Also, maybe we should talk with Jim O'Connor and have him start doing the legal research to see what we can and cannot do."

"I've already spoken with Jim. He basically said since the hospital is legally owned by the directors, just about anything the directors decide would be legal, providing they fully exercise their fiduciary responsibilities to the hospital. So I don't think we have that as an out or stalling tactic."

"Shit! If we thought the Stallworth incident was a public relations nightmare wait until the community hears about this. It is really going to hit the fan. Such is life in the health care industry in the 90's. I guess there isn't a whole lot we can do now until we get the papers. OK Naomi I'll hold tight, I'm sure the phone will be ringing off the hook tomorrow. Keep me informed."

"I think that's right Jack. Try not to be too hard on the students after hearing this."

"I'll probably give the remainder all 'A's' so I won't have to deal with any bitching." They both laughed. But Jack knew that this could be the last laugh he would have for awhile.

Damn, he said to himself as he hung up the telephone. This could not have come at a worse time. He was in his tenure year and wanted to complete the three papers he was writing and submit them for publication before his review came up. He also had to prepare his dossier and tenure statement as well as get letters of evaluation from five outside reviewers. All of these had to be submitted to the tenure committee by next September 15. It was going to be a busy and stressful year. Maybe he and his wife Gabriella could take a nice long special vacation next summer. They had talked about going to Italy. Next week he'll look into some tours and flights. Yea it would be great to get away and spend some time with Gabriella. Jack picked up the next paper to grade.

*****

Over the course of his three years on the Board of Directors of Midland General and the last two years as Board President Jack came to know and respect Dr. Rose. Brent Rose was an impressive man; standing about 5'11" and a still fit 225 pounds, his playing weight when he was throwing touchdown passes for the Midland State Cougars. He had dark black hair that he wore combed straight back and deep black eyes that made him look more like a Mafia hit man rather than a respected surgeon. When he gave you his stare it seemed as if his eyes were piercing the depth of your soul. Originally from Cincinnati he was the only child of a wealthy land developer and entrepreneur. His father, Amerigo

Rossi, was the epitome of a self made man. Amerigo's father always said that a man must have a trade and land. At the age of 13 Brent's father learned barbering at the Franciscan Monastery. He left his homeland of Calabria, Italy when he was 19 years old and settled in Cincinnati where his piasani took him under their wings. He changed his name to Ricky Rose because he thought an American sounding name would be better for business. He heeded his father's advice and invested in land on the outskirts of the city and then developed strip shopping malls. By the time he opened his fourth mall he had acquired sufficient wealth to give up barbering. Looking for a new adventure and excitement he began selling faux jewelry on early morning television in the pre-infomercial days. Though he himself was not educated the elder Rose valued quality education. He enrolled his son in St. Xavier a college preparatory high school where Brent went on to earn all state honors as a quarterback. Though he was recruited by the big name schools- Ohio State, Notre Dame, Michigan and USC these schools thought he was too short to play major league football as a quarterback and wanted him to convert to a defensive back. Midland State was the only big time school to promise him a shot at quarterback. He proved his coaches correct. He was the first freshman to start for the Cougars.

As a junior he was named All-America and led the Cougars to their first, and only, undefeated season and Rose Bowl victory. Most of the sport pundits were touting him for the Heisman or a first round draft pick if he chose to apply for hardship status. But all of that changed the first week of fall practice. A freshman linebacker wanting to impress the coaches either ignored the black jersey or didn't know what it meant and delivered a helmet blow to an unsuspecting and thus unprepared left knee. The jar and subsequent twisting did extensive damage and put an end to the season and ultimately career of Brent Rose quarterback. Ironically the freshman linebacker who delivered the blow went on to play for the Oakland Raiders.

Accepting his fate, Rose graduated with a double major in Business Management and Chemistry, married his college sweetheart and local girl, Jill. In September Jill gave birth to a daughter two weeks before he entered the Medical School in Indianapolis. After his internship at Midland General he accepted a surgical residency with Massachusetts General. Upon completion of the residency he was offered positions in Philadelphia, Boston, Cleveland and Chicago but along with Jill decided to return to Midland. They thought life in a small college town and being close to grandparents would afford them and by now their three daughters a better quality of life. Once again he made the right choice. Perhaps it was his business school training or quarterback mentality, but he became a high risk taker and like his father an entrepreneur. He thrived on competition and would accept nothing less than first place. While he himself was highly intelligent and well informed, he sought out the best consultants and advisors money could buy. Not only was he smart enough to hire good talent he was also smart enough to know when they were bullshitting him and when they were for real; and smart enough to listen to them. It was upon such advice that he built and owns the major out patient surgery center in the southern part of the state and a world-class birthing center. Of course both of these had to be built on a 100 acre parcel of land and the remaining space sold to other physician groups creating a large medical park which is now the hub of outpatient de-livery services in the tri-county area, and a hospital competitor. The large physician group he formed and chaired, Premier, now controlled about 25% of all hospital admissions. Following his father's lead he parlayed his inheritance and land deals to be-come one of the wealthiest men in the state. He was cocky, brash, arrogant, intelligent and wealthy; a combination of talents that made him a formidable opponent.

As Jack hung up the phone he could not stop think-ing about what this all would mean. The news struck him squarely between the eyes. He knew that it would be inevitable that someone would make some offer for affiliation or merger but he did not quite expect this. He knew that any offer from Rose was legitimate and that Rose would treat the hospi-tal fairly but he would play hardball. Jack also knew Rose's primary motive was his own self interest. His thoughts ranged from justifying the offer as at least coming from local physicians and not an out-side group to knowledge that this would dramati-cally change the organization and structure of the

Hospital. One thing was certain, the year 2000 had arrived. The community debate and cries over this were going to be loud and fierce. He knew any proposal to sell the Hospital would not be popular. The *Herald* would have a field day with this. He really wasn't convinced that this would be such a bad deal. The community would still have local control, whatever that meant. Having physicians in control may mean the docs would be more cost conscious. It would not be the first hospital to be owned by physicians. He knew there would be winners and losers, the question was: would the community be a winner or a loser? Oh well, at least there is some time to think things out.

He returned to grading papers and an hour later left for home. On the drive Jack could not help but think about what changing the hospital from a non-profit to a for profit facility would mean to the quality and delivery of medical care in the community that he had adopted as his home since coming here six years ago. He entered his house, threw his keys on the table, scanned the mail and noticed some messages on his machine. "Hey Jack this is your sister give me a call when you can." And there was the usual one "Mr. Victor this is Shell Oil with a courtesy call, we will call back at a later time have yourself a pleasant day." And one that Jack was halfway expecting: "Mr. Victor this is Debra at Dr. Rose's office please call us Monday morning. Dr. Rose would like to meet with you, thank you." Jack wondered what that was all about. Obviously he wanted to talk about the offer but what? He began to guess about the substance of the meeting. Rose has never requested a private meeting with Jack during the past two years that he has chaired the Board- why now- surely it had something to do with the planned offer but beyond that Jack was at loss to find a reason for the private meeting. Jack could never have dreamt what would follow. He went to his bar and poured himself a double Scotch.

During dinner, Jack was unusually quiet. His wife, Gabriella asked what was wrong. Gabriella and Jack had been married for five years and she knew not to probe when he got into one of his quiet moods. But this seemed different. Jack seemed extremely worried and usually did not have a drink before dinner. She asked again- "Jack what's bothering you, you seem very stressed?"

"I got a call from Hoag today. She had a visit from Rook. Premier is going to make a formal offer to buy the Hospital. They want an answer by the next board meeting. I don't know what to do. This is going to be messy."

"You always said the Hospital would have to align with some group."

"Yea, but it is tough when it really happens. The community is really going to be up in arms about this deal. Most of the community leaders dislike Rose, and the rest don't trust him. They see this as an increase the wealth scheme. I was hoping that we would have done more education of the community on the changes in health care, and why the hospital can not stand alone. The timing could not be worse."

"But is there anything you can do? Can the hospital stop him? What happens if you don't sell?"

"I don't know. I guess he can strike a deal with some other hospital. I know he has talked about expanding into William County. If he does then Premier can really put the screws to the hospital. With the Indianapolis groups to the north, and Premier south Midland would be effectively surrounded. Referrals could easily bypass Midland and go to Indianapolis. If that happens down the tubes go all the advanced stuff like cardiovascular, neural, and our attempts to attract a neo-natalogist. Secondary physicians will lose their referral base and most likely leave town. So much for my day; how did things go for you at school today?"

After dinner Jack tried to grade some more papers, but the telephone kept interrupting his thought. Members of the board were calling. Somehow the word had leaked that Premier was about to tender a formal offer to purchase. Board members wanted information that Jack did not have. All he could say was that it appeared to be true that Premier will make an offer. He does not know any content yet. However, he told each that life in the next two years will be entirely different for all involved.

Needless to say, Jack did not get much sleep that weekend. He kept thinking of whether or not this was a good thing for the Hospital and the community. He pondered the question that he would be asked in the upcoming months. How would he respond?

He got out of bed early Monday and arrived at his office about 7:30. He called Rose's office.

"Good morning, Jack Victor calling for Dr. Rose"

"Just a minute please."

"Jack thanks for calling back so soon. I wonder if we could meet for lunch tomorrow - say 12:30 at the Knife and Spoon."

"Let me see- sounds good, Brent, I get out of class at 10:45, no problem. I'll meet you there."

"Good see you there, bye."

*****

Jack felt good to be in the classroom. It was the one place where his mind did not wonder about the sale. Ironically the topic for today's lecture was integrated health systems. Even though he enjoyed what he was doing he found it difficult not to have his mind wonder about the upcoming meeting with Rose He so wanted to talk about the problems of hospitals selling to other organizations and the pressures being placed on hospitals but he knew he couldn't. The students knew of his involvement on the board and would see through the transparent disguise. Class went faster than he wanted. It was now time to leave the safe environment of the classroom and face Rose.

On the way to the restaurant he though about how he would respond if asked to give an opinion on the sale of the hospital. The short trip seemed even shorter this time.

Rose was a large and impressive man. He was aggressive constantly on the offense. His approach to a situation was to over power the opposition, face the situation head on, take quick action and face the consequences whatever they may be. He was also a person of vision. He knew full well what the future of health care was. He knew the hospital could not stand alone. He developed Premier to retain some local control over the manner and type of services delivered in the community. Jack also knew that being a Surgeon, Brent was doing this in part to protect his referrals and the backsides of the other specialists in town. Of course the fact that he could make a profit on the deal did not hurt either. Brent was instrumental in developing the medical arts complex east of town. He also formed the doctors into a network. Jack liked Rose. He was impressed with his effectiveness and vision, and his get it done attitude. Jack wasn't sure if this was an attribute developed from his days on the football field or his training as a surgeon, but Brent dealt with situations head on. One thing about Rose he stated his position told you where he stood and let the chips fall where they may.

Jack arrived at the restaurant a little early and to his surprise, Brent was already there seated at a corner isolated booth with Rook. Adam Rook was a trauma specialist and head of the large trauma group in town that later merged with Premier. He was the antithesis of Rose. Short stocky and non-athletic but highly intelligent and crafty. Most likely in high school he was the class nerd. Quiet but crafty, around the hospital he was known as someone you did not want to cross. He had a reputation for being easily angered and very vindictive; he never saw a grudge he forgot. He lived the mantra- "Don't forget, get even." While Victor respected Rose he did not much trust nor like Rook.

"Good afternoon gentlemen, my name is Sheila, may I get you something to drink before you order?"

Jack usually avoided a drink at lunch but today he thought he might need something. "I'll have a Molson please."

"Same for me."

Brent and Jack spoke about local sports and the Cougars next game. Jack was wondering when Brent would get to the point. Surely, he was not invited to lunch to talk about the Cougars next football game. Rose gave no indication of what his objective for the lunch was, like a quarterback on a naked bootleg he kept the ball close to his hip. Jack ordered a pork tenderloin sandwich with fries; Rose had a large cheeseburger and onion rings while Rook ordered a chicken salad. After they finished the lunch Brent began to get serious.

"Jack, you know we are about to make an offer to buy the hospital. You know why we have to do this. There is no way in hell that we can let those bastards in Indianapolis come to Midland and tell us how to practice medicine. And you know damn well that if we don't get our act together that's exactly what will happen. It is important that this deal go through. Rook and I are building a major system here, and you know that we will be big. You know I do not get involved with losers, hate to lose. Shit, we're gonna be a major player or not play, the hospital can also be a major player or they can sit on the sidelines and be a vendor of services- either way. As one who loves the hospital and wants to see it remain strong I hope you will recommend that the Hospital Board accept our offer- which will be fair. We're not out to screw the hospital. Jack I hope I can count on your support."

Jack responded, "Brent I know the hospital has to change. Pressures from payers will force us to change. But frankly I'm not sure this is the best route. There is a great deal of risk involved as you know. Also the hospital, I think, has some options.

I've already got some questions about why we don't merge with University in Indianapolis. Whatever decision the board makes it will take a lot of flak from the community and from other physicians. You know..."

Rose interrupted and reacted as Jack had anticipated "Damn it! Jack nothing is worth doing if you can't take the heat. It's about time the board got some balls and quit trying to please everybody. You and I both don't want to see medical care controlled by outsiders. This is our last hope for local control. Also if health care costs are gonna be managed, the system has to be under the control of physicians. We are the ones on the line. We're the ones who can effectively make the decisions. This is what we have built and you and I both know this is the wave of the future and the way the hospital should move. The sooner the board wakes up to this the better for everybody."

With that Rose did something that took Jack by surprise. He asked Rook to give Jack a small package.

"What's this?"

"Consider it a consulting fee. Premier would like you to give a short lecture on- let us say the role of for profit hospitals. Jack we need your support on this. Consider that the first part of a 'consulting fee' for your help in getting the hospital to see the light and do the right thing for itself and the community.

Think about it, you and I know this is what needs to be done. Deliver the votes and another envelope will be waiting."

Jack was in a state of shock, completely speechless but before Jack could respond and as if it were planned, Brent's beeper went off. Rose pulled out his cellular and made a call. "Ok be right there, I'm on my way. Sorry Jack need to get to the office. Think about what I said." With that Rose laid down $50.00 on the table and he and Rook excused themselves.

Jack sat there in astonishment at what had happened, he just stared at the package and ordered another Molson. His ethics and moral principles raced through his mind. In the privacy of his car he opened the package and counted one hundred one hundred dollar bills, with a typed note "Other ten due upon completion of project".

*****

On the way back to the office from the Knife and Spoon restaurant all Jack thought about was lunch and what had happened. "Shit, I just took a bribe. But what's the real harm in working as an agent? Perhaps this is in the best interest of the hospital and community anyway." Rose was a powerful and persuasive man. He could get people to commit to things without their realizing what had happened. Victor observed this once when in a public forum, Rose announced that the managed care company that won the local contract agreed to donate 5% of their profits back to the community. Of course this was news to the CEO of the managed care organization, all he could say was "it's a way for our organization to be a responsible citizen". He was caught with his proverbial pants down.

On the other hand, Jack thought selling out to Premier was in the best interest of the hospital and perhaps the community. Most likely it would ensure the survivability of the hospital and keep medical care local. Also since being part of a coordinated system was within the strategic plan of the hospital the proposal was not too far out of line with the direction the board wanted to move. The board had already been sensitized to the fact that integration could be inevitable. So as Victor rationalized his own action, he reasoned that if he could persuade the board to accept the offer from Premier this would indeed be in the best interests of the community and the hospital, and if he could make a buck off the deal so be it. After all his role as a board member was to ensure the survivability of the hospital. Given the hospital's financial situation selling the hospital might after all be in the best interests of the hospital and the community.

Jack Victor entered his office and turned on the computer to check his messages. The usual student requests for information about the final exam, notes from Laura about funding opportunities, and a phone message that Greg Martinelli had called and wanted Jack to call back.

Martinelli was a member of the board and president of one of the local banks. Though they did not know each other before Martinelli's coming onto the board two years before, Jack and Greg became close. Martinelli was a master at finances and knew this aspect of the business cold in fact he was appointed to the board because of his savvy of financial issues. During the Finance Committee meetings they would sit next to each other and Greg would explain the meaning of the various ratios to Jack, while Jack explained the meaning of the various health care acronyms to Greg. They often joked about this mutual education role.

"Greg, Jack here, I got your message."

"Jack, thanks for calling back so quickly. I'd really like to have lunch with you as soon as possible. How does your calendar look?"

"Just so happens I'm open tomorrow, that o.k.? You want to meet me at Second Bow?"

"No that is a bit crowded let's go some place out a ways where we can talk."

"Ok Greg, how about Bibbs on South Walnut about noon."

"Sounds good-see you then."

Now what was that all about Jack pondered surely it had to do with the sale.

*****

The next day Jack met Greg Martinelli at the restaurant. Greg was already seated when Jack arrived. When the waitress came to give both men menus, Jack said he would have the usual; a Reuben, fried onion rings and a large ice tea. Greg ordered the BLT, Cole slaw and a diet cola.

"So Jack, what do think the Cougars chances are on Saturday?"

"A lot depends on Miller's gimpy ankle. If he can't play we don't have much of a running game and that means they can double Carty. Solomon is a good passer but he can't run worth a darn and if you switch to Sampson you lose the passer and do not gain speed."

"Yea- deceptively slow. Sometimes I think we should nickname Sampson 'Funnel Cloud'—a lot of wind, but no touchdown. Sure would be nice to win the last two and go to the Rose Bowl."

"The best part would be beating those boys up north and getting the Governor's Trophy back. There are too many "P's" on that thing to suit me. But as much as you and I like football you didn't invite me to lunch to discuss the season. Wanna talk about the sale offering?"

"You got it Jack. That's about all I've been able to think about. I looked at the numbers, met with Vern and the deal is not a bad deal from a financial point; especially given our census and operating margin numbers the past few months. But I just have an uneasy feeling about turning over what is tantamount to a community asset to Rose and his boys. Is it a good idea to have him control the hub of medical care in this community- I don't know?"

"Greg, I'm pretty much in the same boat. My concern is how are the docs going to get around the Stark regulations? They're going to have to watch their referral patterns pretty closely. The only out I see is that from what I learned Rose has put together a syndicate that has five physicians and ten non-physicians, mostly from up north, to buy the hospital. So given that I guess they technically meet the Stark rules. In executive committee we often talked about what a difference it would make if the docs were spending their own dollars; maybe they wouldn't be asking for the latest technology all the time"

"That's a good point, between you and me I'm not sure how I will vote."

Suddenly Jack felt in the midst of an ethical dilemma. He remembered the money in the envelope and how a simple word here might sway Greg's vote and get Jack off the hook. Instead he just nodded and said "Yea, me too."

*****

After lunch Jack went back to campus. He found it more and more difficult to concentrate on the lecture topic. His mind kept going back to the meeting with Rose and Rook. He knew there was no way he could keep the money but how would he get himself out of the current predicament? He felt a bit intimidated by Rose and quite frankly feared Rook. He had heard the rumors about his violent temper.

As fate would have it, the case for discussion in today's health ethics seminar was whether or not it was ethical for a hospital CEO to accept transportation and tickets to the super bowl from a vendor. Once or twice he almost had a slip of the tongue and instead of super bowl tickets he almost said cash.

After class he hurried back to the sanctity of his office and prepared for the three-thirty faculty meeting. He detested faculty meetings, as did most of his colleagues. But being untenured he wanted to make sure he did all he could to gain tenure points. He couldn't understand how a group of highly intelligent individuals who taught executive decision making could spend so much time debating an issue and arguing over the smallest detail. He almost got up and left the meeting last year when they spent ninety minutes arguing if the grade point average for admission to the school should be 2.3 or 2.5. All though that meeting he kept telling himself what difference does .2 points make? Why not compromise and make it 2.4? Today's meeting would be equally lengthy. The only action item on the agenda is a proposal to change the general education requirements to include at least four semesters of a foreign language. This proposal is being advanced by the political science faculty. It was a sure thing that whatever the poli-sci group pushed for the economics faculty would argue against. If the faculty decided to serve chocolate ice cream at the faculty staff picnic you can count on the econ group to argue for vanilla.

At three thirty nine the dean opened the meeting. After a few general information items, he opened the floor for consideration of the proposed change to the general education requirements. As Jack had anticipated the political science coalition started to push for the change. Arguing that our world is shrinking, we need to globalize, our students should know more about other cultures etc. Of course the economists argued that our students are mathematical illiterate and if any changes were to be made in the general education requirements it should be to add more higher level math courses. The arguments went back and forth but Jack couldn't tell you much of what transpired. He sat there with his notepad and doodled "20,000=aye, 0=nay" He kept drawing circles on the page while his mind flipped from considering the sale a good deal for the hospital and the community to one that will most likely create a medical care monopoly. He thought about what Greg had said that this was a way out of the red ink. What to do? How to vote?

Finally after a very lengthy discussion the issue was

up for a vote. The dean asked all those in favor of the change in general education to say aye. A chorus of ayes could be heard. Those opposed nay; an equally loud chorus of nays.

"Any abstentions?" Jack responded by saying "Abstain".

"Seems the ayes carry the day. Motion to add four semesters of a foreign language to the general education requirements passes. We are now adjourned."

Was this an omen of things to come?

Chapter 2
The Alliance

Leon Crowe went to the school's Human Resource Department to review Jack's tenure dossier. As a colleague he was expected to review each candidate for tenure's case and cast a yes or no vote. In Crowe's case he was not only a colleague in the school but also a member of the Promotion and Tenure Committee. As a faculty member in Jack's school his opinion would carry a great deal of influence with other P & T members. But Leon was reviewing Jack's dossier not to find the strong points to argue in support of Jack's case, but rather weaknesses. While Leon and Jack were colleagues in the same school they were hardly friends or even allies.

He was the example of the proverbial "tall, dark and handsome" man. He used his appearance to his advantage. Among the faculty he had the reputation as a "womanizer". He always managed to be assigned the most attractive female as his graduate assistant. His third wife filed for divorce after she discovered him having an affair with a graduate student. Since both were "consenting adults" and the girl involved was not a student in Leon's school and thus he had no supervisory control over her it was technically not sexual harassment. But it did constitute grounds for a divorce. He was already on the prowl a month after the divorce was filed.

An Econometrician, Leon Crowe was extremely conservative and a staunch fundamentalist. He had argued that a program in health administration, or any other specialty area, was inappropriate in a school of public affairs. His argument was that the school should focus only on general public administration courses as found in traditional schools of public administration and not offer special interest majors such as health, or poverty, or non-profit management. He constantly argued that such programs diffused limited and finite resources from the school's core mission. Because of his views he became an adversary and fought Jack on every issue. Sometimes Jack felt Crowe's attacks to be more personal rather than professional.

Since Jack built the health administration program into the second largest major in the school, Leon knew that the faculty would never vote to eliminate a cash cow. He saw Jack's bid for tenure and promotion as an opportunity to get rid of his foe. Thus he was looking for ammunition to argue that Jack

Victor not be granted tenure and thus in essence fired. He believed that with Jack gone he could sabotage the program and the major would fail on its merits.

He knew that Jack would make a strong argument for tenure based on his excellent teaching performance. Since Jack's teaching evaluation scores were among the highest in the school an attack on teaching criteria would not get Leon very far. Furthermore, if Jack completed his textbook and articles in process his research record would also be difficult to challenge. Leon was hoping to find some less than satisfactory performance in the area of service- the third criterion necessary for promotion and tenure. Thus a call to Naomi Hoag would be his first step.

*****

After he finished reviewing Jack's file Leon returned to his office and called Naomi Hoag. He hoped that she could give him some information to challenge his service record.

Bonnie answered the phone with her usual cheery "Good afternoon, Ms. Hoag's office this is Bonnie how may I help you?"

"Good afternoon this is professor Crowe and I would like to speak with Ms. Hoag."

After a brief pause Naomi Hoag took the call. Leon

explained that he was a member of the university promotion and tenure committee and asked if he could meet her in the near future to obtain her assessment of Jack's performance as a hospital board member and president of the board of directors. He asked her if the two could meet sometime to discuss Jack's contributions to the hospital and the board of directors.

"Professor Crowe I will be very happy to meet with you but my calendar is full the next few days. We currently have the state board of health inspectors here for the annual audit and then the JCAHO team will be visiting for the accreditation review. Would you be willing to meet in the evening some time?"

"That would be fine with me. The committee does need to have the documents ready for review fairly quickly." Leon knew this was not true but wanted to hear what Naomi had to tell him so he could try to get a less favorable review from someone else should her comments prove beneficial to Jack's case.

Naomi also wanted to find out what Crowe's side in Jack's case was so she also wanted to meet as soon as possible. "Fine then can we meet Tuesday evening? Say at 7:30 and if you don't mind we can meet at my condo? The inspectors will be in the hospital and besides it will be more comfortable then at the office."

"Sure time is ok with me. What's the address?"

"It's unit 18 in the Summit Ridge subdivision off of South Kent Avenue."

"I know exactly where that is. It's just south of the Little League fields."

"Correct. I'll see you at 7:30"

When Naomi hung up the phone she thought that this might be a golden opportunity. Naomi's ex-husband was a finance professor at Central Florida University thus she was very familiar with the tenure process. She knew that denial of a tenure request was tantamount to a termination. Over the past few months tensions between her and Jack Victor began to surface. She had some serious differences with the path the board was taking especially in looking at possible affiliation with an Indianapolis hospital system. Her knowledge of the university process and Machiavellian character quickly saw this as a potential way to at least embarrass Jack Victor and at best have his contract with the university not renewed.

Crowe hung up the phone and with a wry smile on his face gathered up his lecture notes and headed off to teach V540 Governmental Budgeting and Finance

*****

Tuesday evening at 7:35 Leon Crowe arrived at unit 18 in the Summit Ridge subdivision and rang the door bell. A short time later Naomi Hoag opened the door and invited the professor in. Crowe was startled to see her. He had not expected such an attractive woman. She was a stunning lady with a very good figure. Crowe's first thought was that he had wished this was a social rather than a professional meeting. Hoag was also impressed by the good looks of Leon Crowe. He looked nothing like her ex-husband's colleagues at CFU.

After exchanging greetings and a polite handshake Naomi asked Leon to take a seat on the couch. She also asked him if he would like a glass of Cabernet.

"Love to; thank you for the offer."

After pouring two glasses she took a seat on the couch next to Leon. Leon went on to explain the tenure and promotion process in excruciating detail and the need the committee had for the outside reviews of the candidate's performance in the three major areas- teaching, research, and service. Even though Naomi was fully aware of the process, having shared the experience with her ex-husband, she listened very attentively as if she were interested in Leon's ramblings. While she listened her thoughts kept returning to the physical attributes of the man sitting next to her.

"Thank you for the explanation, Leon. I will of course provide the committee with a fair assessment of Jack's service to the hospital. I will send you something in a week or two. Is that soon enough?"

As she was talking Leon too was taken by the attractiveness of the hospital CEO. He thought for a woman of her age she was quite the looker. Hell he thought, she was good looking at any age. Leon's thoughts returned to the issue at hand.

"Great. Sure a week or two will be fine. By the way, Jack has waived his right to review outside documents so whatever you write will only be seen by the committee members and not revealed to Jack." He added the last comment in the hopes hat if she had something damaging to say she would be more likely to mention those things in her review. "If you like you may address the letter to me and send it to my office."

The two had some more wine and engaged in small talk. She asked, as if interested, in Leon's area of research and the courses he taught even though she was distracted by his handsomeness. In turn Leon was listening to her small talk about how she arrived at Midland and her past jobs.

Finally Leon decided to make a move. He gently put his left arm on her shoulder. She did not object. He then began to gently move his hand over her shoulder. This time she moved closer and put her head on his shoulder. She raised her head and their eyes locked onto each other. As their heads became closer their lips touched lightly. She moved away briefly and then kissed him; this time a passionate and long kiss. After the kiss she got up from the couch took his hand and led him into the bed room.

*****

The next day Leon Crowe was sitting at his kitchen table finishing his second cup of coffee. He put the *Herald* aside and began to think about the previous night. A smile came across his face. What a grand night. Not only did he have great sex with a good looking woman, but also he found an ally in his efforts to get Jack's tenure case denied. From his talking with Naomi, especially in the bedroom, he sensed from her tone and the careful words that she used that she too would like to see Jack Victor leave Midland.

Feeling pretty good with his night's accomplishments he got up from the table, got in his red Corvette and headed off to campus.

Meanwhile, in unit 18 in the Summit Ridge subdivision Naomi Hoag was also getting ready for her day at the hospital. However, her thoughts were more on Leon Crowe as Jack's adversary rather than the bedroom activities. She knew that Crowe also wanted to see Jack Victor leave Midland, though she was not quite sure why. It didn't matter. As long as she had one ally on the committee she did not care about motives.

On the drive to the hospital she was thinking how she could word her letter so as not to give Jack a favorable review. After all, his performance as a board member was very good. And even though she disagreed with the direction the hospital was headed and other issues she had to confess that Jack did show good leadership. The challenge would be to carefully craft the letter so as to leave ambiguity in the committee members' minds. Oh well, at least she had some time to work on it. Today's challenge would be getting through the first day of the JCAHO accreditation visit. She knew one of the three auditors from a previous review at another hospital. Seems he was more interested in fidelity to his wife rather than momentary pleasure. Their meeting again should be interesting to say the least.

*****

Billie Franklin sat in the last row but his mind kept wandering and he was thoroughly bored with Professor Crowe's discussion of beta weights. He knew there was no way he would be able to pass this course. A failing grade and he most likely would be expelled from the program, and maybe the university. This was already his ninth semester as an undergraduate and he still needed to pass forty-eight more credit hours for his undergraduate degree. Even though he knew Crowe was a hard-ass and not about to cut a floundering undergraduate any slack; he still decided to visit the professor during office hours and make a plea for some leniency.

*****

An hour later the student arrived at the office of Professor Crowe. There already was a short line waiting to see the teacher. Franklin thought it fortunate to be at the end of the line and thus his conversation not likely to be overheard by another student. Finally it was his turn. He meekly entered the office and was greeted with a harsh "Sit Down! What favor do you want?"

Franklin knew how to play the system and he knew now was not the time for brashness but a show of humility. He took a seat and gave the usual excuses for his poor performance- need to work two jobs just to pay tuition and how even though his grades did not reveal it, he enjoyed Macro-Economics and may want to pursue a career in the econ field. Of course Crowe heard this many times before and knew it was a line of b.s. After the student had rested his case Crowe said something unexpected.

"OK ok I tell you what. I don't know why but I have confidence in you. I'll give you an 'I' for the course and you can repeat it with me next semester. The 'I' will save you some tuition dollars. Now unless you want something else I'm pretty busy."

"No no, thank you so much. Of course I will take the incomplete and promise you that I will do better next semester. Thank you again, professor, and if there is any thing I can do for you let me know."

"You're welcome and if I need some help in the future I will let you know."

With that the student gathered his things and left the office. He was surprised that he had been given a break and wondered what was meant by some future obligation. Oh well at least the incomplete will keep him in school for another semester. He'll worry about any re-payment later. Maybe some grading or library gopher work. It'll be worth it for the "I".

Crowe closed the door to his office, not sure why he gave that kid a break and the reason for the "if I need a favor I'll call" remark. He began to ponder the telephone call he took before office hours from the chairman of the school's P & T committee to tell him that Jack Victor's pre- tenure year dry run went very well and that if he completed the pending work he most likely will sail through the committee. The chair wanted to share this with his colleague. Of course unknowingly to the chair Leon did not find such news as particularly good news. He sat at his desk thinking that if Jack got tenure then the chances of getting rid of his foe are nil. He kept coming back to the idea that Jack needed to be dealt with outside the tenure process. Maybe he could rid himself of Jack Victor before the tenure decision- but how?

Chapter 3
The Meeting

Jack Victor did not sleep well for the past two weeks since the Rose proposal. Today was no exception. He awoke around four thirty restless and unable to get back to sleep he got up and went to the kitchen to fix a pot of extra strong coffee. He poured a cup and walked to the set of French doors. He looked out at the yard now covered with a layer of snow. The white canvas of snow lying on the field was only dotted by the footprints of a deer. It was the kind of snow Jack enjoyed- just enough to cover the ground but not enough to make driving hazardous. Were it not for the pending board meeting he most likely would have taken a long walk in the woods. He thought to himself, if only about eight inches had fallen the roads would have been impassable and the meeting called off. He sat in a lounge chair in the family room sipping on his coffee and watching a rerun of Sports Center, but his mind was on the event about to take place at ten this morning. He knew that whichever way the vote came out, he would be the scapegoat. He would also be known as the board president who sold out the hospital to a private interest group.

Around seven Gabriella came down and gave him a kiss and asked if he wanted some breakfast.

"Yea, maybe some Scotch"

"Too early for that but I can fix you some pancakes or French toast. Given what day it is I may even let you have some bacon."

"Thanks, but my stomach is in no shape for food."

Jack sat there for quite awhile, then took a long shower and got dressed for the meeting.

"Good luck, see you for dinner."

"Thanks, I love you."

*****

The drive from the lake house to the hospital usually took about 40 minutes; but that day it seemed as if he arrived at the parking garage in no time. As he pulled into the parking spot reserved for the board president and turned off the ignition he sat for a moment took a deep breath and said "What the hell. Might as well walk into the fires of hell sooner rather than later."

He walked up the back stairs to the second floor and the board room. "Good morning Mr. Victor" said Bonnie. "It's gonna be an eventful meeting to say the least. Want a cup of coffee, I just brewed a pot?"

"No thanks, Bonnie. I think I already had my fill for the day."

As he entered the board room most of the directors were already there. He spotted Drs. Joseph and Lincoln talking with Pam Summers. Joseph would surely vote his conscience. A very ethical person Dr. Joseph would most likely argue against the sale on ethical grounds.

Lincoln was the medical chief of staff. Elected by his peers he is well respected for his no nonsense approach and sense of fairness. Pam Summers would most likely vote with the doctors. Rarely did she do otherwise.

Naomi Hoag came up to Jack and said that Ronald Jefferson left a message that he would not be at to-day's meeting. He has a conflict in Indianapolis. Jack said "Not surprising. Jefferson never seems to be able to make a controversial meeting." But Jack also knew that this meant eight voting members present rather than the odd number nine, which if the vote came down to a tie, he would be responsible for casting the deciding vote. Something he did not want to do. "Let's get started."

"O.K everybody let's get started. If you take a seat we will start the meeting. For the minutes I will ask the secretary to call the roll."

Bonnie begins the roll call of directors.

"Dr. Joseph?"

"Here"

"Dr. Lincoln?"

"Here"

"Dr. Jewell?"

"Present"

"Mr. French?"

"Here"

"Mr. Jefferson is absent.

Mr. Martinelli?"

"Here"

"Ms. Ranier?"

"Here"

"Ms. Summers?"

"Here"

"Mrs. Twist?"

"Present"

"Mr. Victor?"

"Here, let the minutes show that all are present with the exception of Mr. Jefferson. For the record this is a special meeting of the Hospital Board for the sole purpose of considering acceptance or rejection of the proposal from Premier to purchase the hospital and its assets for a total sum of $86 million dollars. I believe you all had an opportunity to review the documents Naomi sent to all of us. Naomi anything you would like to add?"

"No Jack, I think it is straight forward. Administration I believe has exercised its due diligence in reviewing the particulars. We will not be offering a recommendation. At this time I would like to ask our CFO Vern Dailey to review the particulars with you, Vern."

Dailey went on to explain the financing structure and how the total sale price would be spread over a five year period with semi-annual payments. The total amount would be deposited into a community based fund managed by a board of trustees; the sole purpose of the funds would be to finance medical care for indigent and other low-income noninsured individuals. He concluded his remarks by saying that the offer was comparable to the purchase price paid for the Warren County Hospital. After fielding some general questions Vern gave the floor back to Jack.

"OK, I guess the moment is here. To make this in line with Roberts Rules I will need a motion to accept the Premier proposal. I think it would be easier if the motion be phrased as a positive i. e. to accept so as to avoid a double negative and thus easier to vote. Anyone care to go out on a limb?"

After a pause, Terri Rainier spoke up, "I move that the board accept the proposal from Premier to purchase Midland General and its assets for the sum of $86 million dollars and hereby incorporate their offer in this motion."

"Do I hear a second?"

"Second" by Dr. Lincoln

"It has been moved and seconded that we accept the offer. The floor is now open for discussion."

Mary Twist was the first to speak, but it was not what Jack wanted to hear. "I would like to amend the motion to read that the board will consider the issue after a sufficient number of public forums are held to assess what the community wants us to do."

"I second" said Pam Summers

"Looks like we have an amendment and a second, we're now ready for discussion of the amendment."

"I'd like to offer some background."

"Go ahead Naomi."
"As you know the *Herald* has run a series of articles on the offer. Cassie still has some inside contacts at the paper and told me that e-mails, phone messages and letters have been running about 50/50. So whatever the outcome half of the community is gonna be pissed."

Greg Martinelli gave some more insight. "You know these forums will be heated and I think this will put the board in a no win situation. If sentiment is running 50/50 it seems to me that there is not a clear majority either way. Stating the obvious this tells me that whatever way we go a large proportion of the community is going to accuse us of not listening to public input. If Cassie is right I see no gain coming from having forums."

Jim O'Connor virtually put a halt to further discussion- "May I remind the board that it only has until next Wednesday to make a decision. Then Rose and his syndicate will pull the offer. It would not surprise me if this is not what he is hoping we do, and then he can feel free to build a competing hospital just as he did with the surgery center. From some of his past comments about the board and administration I believe he wants to build and run his own facility."

With that Summers withdrew her second.

"We now have a motion with no second, anyone care to second Mary's motion. Hearing none, then the motion fails for lack of a second. Now back to the original motion Dr. Joseph. You have a comment to make?"

"Yes. I have nothing against Rose or Rook. I think they both are good physicians and do care about medical care in our city. But I feel strongly that this is an unethical proposal. It is unethical, for physicians to have a major ownership role in hospitals. It amounts to self referrals. As physicians we should stick to what we were trained to do- heal sick patients. Leave the business side of medicine to the business folks. I am going to vote against this and I hope you all follow."

Greg Martinelli spoke next, "I'm just a simple small town bank president and really do not know if Dr. Joseph is correct or not as to the ethics of physician ownership, but I think I have a pretty good idea of finances and from a financial standpoint this is a pretty good deal. Rose is not sticking it to us. He has offered a fair price. The money we gain on the sale over time could provide a good source of funding for low income citizens. We could, in a short period of time, be the first community to have a non-governmental form of universal coverage. Right now, unless someone convinces me otherwise, I say we take the deal."

Naomi reminded the board that about six months ago Warren County Hospital in the northern part of the state sold to a proprietary corporation for 100 million dollars.

Terri Ranier, a local CPA and member of the finance committee then gave a short analysis. "Naomi brought up a good point. Warren is licensed for 200 plus beds. Midland is a 170 bed hospital so the offer from Premier is in line with the offer Warren accepted. So the offer is a fair market price. Also, we have experienced large monthly deficits. Our cash reserve fund is dangerously low. We still owe $750,000 for the new MRI. Given recent trends and the proposed Medicare reimbursement cuts, without an infusion of new cash we will be hard pressed to meet current obligations. This sale gives the hospital new monies to sustain itself. I don't think we have any other choice but to accept."

Dr. Joseph responded "Terri, you are correct. However, Warren County was a publicly owned facility and the taxpayers wanted to get out of the hospital business. They had community support, I'm not sure we have that support."

As Jack thought Lincoln sided with his colleague and argued against the proposal. Dr. Jewell who had led a group of physicians calling for the firing of Hoag could not resist the chance to get in his points. "Look, financially this is not a bad deal. Additionally it will allow the new owners the chance to name a new, and hopefully more effective, administration. I agree that hospitals should be under the control of physicians. I say go for the deal!"

The discussion went on for a little over an hour with no clear consensus.

"Anymore comments before I call for the question? Hearing none..."
Before Jack could ask for the ayes and the nays Dr. Joseph called for a roll call vote.

"A roll call vote has been called. Bonnie will you please call the roll? Remember a yes vote is a vote for the proposal to sell and a nay vote means you wish not to sell. Bonnie."

Bonnie began the roll call

Dr. Joseph , "no"

Dr. Lincoln, "no"

Dr. Jewell , "yes"

Mr. French, "no"

Mr. Jefferson is absent

Mr. Martinelli, "yes"

Ms. Ranier , "yes"

Mrs. Pam Summers "yes"

Mrs. Twist, "no

"We have four positive and four negative votes. Mr. Victor how do you vote?"

Victor swallowed hard. Shit he thought this was not what he had hoped for his being the deciding vote. He wanted to vote "abstain" but he knew he could not do that. Racing through his head were thoughts of the 20 grand, the lecture on professional ethics he gave to seniors, and the fact that deep down he thought this might be a good deal for the hospital and the community.

"Mr. Victor"

"I vote aye"

"The motion carries 5 to 4. Thank all of you for your hard work and participation in a most serious decision. The meeting is now adjourned."

*****

Jack did not stay around to talk or to have lunch saying that he had some papers to grade. He wanted to be alone. He picked up his attaché case and exited down the back stairs. On the way back to the office he started to get an aching in his stomach and his palms were sweaty. He started to question the vote that had just been taken. Somewhere in his heart he felt that he made the right decision; but were his motives correct? He questioned not so much the outcome but the process and his role in it. Specifically he thought about the money. If Rose had gotten to Jack maybe he had gotten to other board members. What did he get himself into? Now the nagging thought that he had taken a bribe gnawed at him. At this particular moment he did not like himself. As each car passed by he imagined the occupants asking him "How could you do such a thing?" A question he asked himself a thousand times during the short drive from the hospital to the campus.

He arrived at the office just in time to pick up his notes and head off to class. At least that was an environment in which he could feel some comfort. However, his class that day was an uncommon un-enthusiastic lecture. He concluded the lecture with his signature "Go in peace." He got through it but could not recall anything he taught. He gathered up his stuff and quickly exited. He kept thinking about the envelope and the money in the upper right hand drawer of his office desk.

As he walked down the long hallway he heard a familiar voice "Dr. V. you o.k.?" He stopped turned, and saw Angela one of his students.

"Yes, Ange. Why?"

Angie was a bit older than the traditional college junior; a student who possessed a great deal of insight and knowledge for her years.

"Well you just didn't seem like your self today and I was kinda worried if you were feeling alright."

"No, no I'm fine just that things have been a bit unusually hectic with the sale proposal and all that you have been reading in the paper. Well, I'm o.k."

"Dr. V. I know that the vote was supposed to be taken today. Anything you can tell us? You usually come back from the board meeting pretty enthused and tell us the non-confidential material"

"Nah, nothing is public yet. Hoag needs to inform Dr. Rose before we can release anything to the public. I'll let you know as soon as I can. But thanks for your concern."

With that he left locked the office door and sat quietly in a darkened office.

*****

It was now 2:30 the day after the board meeting and the historic vote. Jack was in the office reading the proposed change to the undergraduate curriculum when the phone rang. "Yes, Jennifer."

"Jack, Ms Hoag is on the line, do you want to take the call?"

"Of course, put her through."

"Jack, well it is done. We signed the purchase papers about an hour ago."

"I'm not surprised, it's what he wanted. What's the time table?"

"The deal is to be closed in about eight months then we will be Premier Midland General Hospital. I guess I'd better send out resumes."

"Naomi there is still the other matter we talked about."

"I know, Jack. I've been thinking about my strategy but with all this sale stuff I have not had much time. Let me get back with you on that in a few weeks. O.K.?"

"I will need to know your decision by next board meeting."

"OK. Bye and I will keep you informed if there are any changes."

"Bye Naomi."

*****

The next morning to no one's surprise the headlines

of the *Herald* read **HOSPITAL SELLS TO PRIEMIER.** The following article contained the press release from Michelle and numerous quotes from Rose and Rook. As Jack had predicted the editorial that day severely criticized the hospital for conducting business behind closed doors and without community input. Hoag only responded by saying that the hospital was a privately owned corporation and thus not subject to sunshine laws. Jack declined to be interviewed and the *Herald* reported that Victor was not available for comment.

Crisis time has begun.

The next day Jack sat in the office reading a journal article and trying to prepare for the next class.

"Jack, a special messenger is here with a package for you and says that you are the only one who can sign for it."

"OK Jennifer have him come to the office."

Victor opened the door and saw the brown uniformed messenger. "You Mr. Jack Victor?"

"Yes"

"Please sign here."

Jack signed the receipt, took the large manila envelope closed the door and sat quietly at his desk. Strange he thought no return address. He needed no more information. He had a good idea who the sender was and its contents. He sat there looking at it. Finally he got the letter opener out of the desk and opened it and to his fear saw the $10, 000 and a computer generated note "Job well done."

The rest of the day was a non-productive waste. He unplugged the phone so as not to be disturbed. He paced the office occasionally picking up the envelope then angrily throwing it back on the desk. How could he have been so weak and stupid to have accepted the first envelope? How did this all happen? It seems the whole mess happened in an instant.

Jack left the office and went down the back stairs to the parking garage. He started for home, but instead stopped at the "Whistling Hole" took a seat at the far end of the bar and ordered a double Scotch on the rocks. He felt like getting drunk, but knew that was no answer. He sat quietly and nursed the drink and avoided eye contact with any of the other patrons. He felt their stares and wondered if they were whispering to each other that he was the man who sold out the hospital. About an hour later he paid his tab and left for the long drive home.

Chapter 4
The Confession

The last few weeks were not easy ones for Jack. He hardly slept, and was unusually irritable. Even the classroom did not provide him much comfort. He did not go on campus except to teach his classes but instead stayed at home ostensibly finishing the textbook he was writing for his tenure review, but all he really was doing was thinking about what had happened and his role in the affair. Gabriella was becoming very concerned. She knew something was upsetting him but every time she asked him and tried to comfort him he would only say "nothing's wrong." Jack knew what was gnawing at him and what he had to do about it.

He also did something that he never did before; he started to drink more heavily during the day. He did not reply to the many e-mail and phone messages he received. One set of messages was from Gary Riggs a reporter at the *Herald* and long time friend of Jack and Gabriella. In fact it was Gary who introduced the two. In college Gary dated her a few times and at a fraternity party introduced her to his friend Jack Victor and shortly after that meeting Riggs was one of the Groomsmen in their wedding. Gary never married and still had a warm spot in his heart for her.

Riggs knew that it was not like Jack not to return his calls. He usually returned calls very promptly. Riggs had always been willing to work with the board and report hospital matters in a fair and impartial way, even though the *Herald*'s editorial board took a somewhat different approach. As a result Jack was open with Riggs and gave him whatever information he could about hospital dealings and issues. The two had a very good relationship that went back to their college days. Riggs knew something was wrong and wondered what caused such a change in behavior. Out of concern, or maybe a bit of hoped for lust, he called Gabriella at her school and arranged to have lunch on Tuesday. Gary knew that something was not right. It was not like Jack to duck publicity. In fact Gary thought that Jack had a bit of ham in him and enjoyed the coverage. He often thought that had Jack not gone into teaching he would be in theatre.

*****

Throughout lunch on Tuesday Gabriella and Gary

exchanged some talk about her teaching. After eating Gary began to talk about his concerns.

"Gabby, I'm concerned about this sale thing and the toll it has taken on Jack. Something does not smell right to me. The whole thing took place too fast. There was no community input, which is not like Jack's approach. If anything he usually sought too much community input. I'm also worried about Jack. He's not returning phone calls and won't speak to me."

"Gary, I'm scared for Jack. Since the vote he has not been himself. You're not alone, he hardly speaks to anyone. We have not had a decent conversation since the vote. Something's eating at him and I can't find out what."

"Gabby, I asked you to meet me because of the friendship I have with you and Jack. And because of this I need to tell you that I am beginning an investigation into the sale and the process in which it took place and I want you to know this and be prepared for what comes out. I have an ethical responsibility to my paper and to the community to report whatever I find."

"I know Gary; you have to do what you must do. I now wish Jack had never accepted appointment to the board. He only did it for the tenure brownie points, but he would most likely have gotten tenure on teaching and research alone. Let me see if I can talk to Jack."

"OK but I need to start on the investigation before things cool down."

With that they both left.

*****

Meanwhile Jack got off the recliner, went to his bar and poured himself a double Scotch. Filling the glass with ice he went back into the family room. Swirling the ice in the tumbler he watched as the cubes slowly rotated and thought to himself this is not right. He knew that his life was going to hell. "I need to do something to rectify things. I can not continue like this. It will wreck my career, my marriage and my life. I've got to do something but what?" He quickly drank the Scotch and poured himself another drink.

Shortly, Gabriella came home and saw Jack sitting in the darkened room, unshaven and with the almost empty glass of Scotch on the end table.

"Jack, you alright?"

"Damn it Gabriella for the last time I'm alright. Quit your God damn nagging."

With that Gabriella knocked the glass out of his hand and on to the floor.

"You're not alright and haven't been since that vote. I've just about had it with your behavior.

Quite frankly I'm about at the end of my rope. Tell me what's wrong or we no longer have a marriage!"

Jack sat there speechless, motionless and seemingly unaware or uncaring about what she said.

"Screw you, I'm going upstairs. See me when you come to your senses."

About an hour later, maybe due to the alcohol wearing off or the fear of losing his marriage Jack got out of his chair and went upstairs. Gabriella was sitting in the bedroom suite reading some and crying a lot. Jack sat next to her quietly for about five minutes. Then he began to tell her the whole story about the lunch the money and the vote.

"My god Jack. Why didn't you tell me sooner?"

"I was too ashamed and embarrassed."

"What do we do now?"

"I've decided that tomorrow I'm gonna call Rook meet him and give him back the money. If I don't I can't live with myself and I now realize you won't be able to live with me either."

She leaned over gave him a kiss and they made love for the first time in weeks.

That night Jack slept better than he had in a long time. He didn't know if the confession to Gabriella or the good sex put his mind at ease, but in any event he was ready for the chore facing him.

*****

Jack got to his office early. He replied to some students' e-mails, read a journal article and at nine o'clock nervously picked up the phone and called Adam Rook. He dialed the first five numbers and then put the receiver down. What was he going to say? How would he tell Rook that he was returning the money? After three attempts, Jack finally got enough nerve to complete the dial.

"Good morning Premier Health Care, how may I help you?"

"Good morning this is Jack Victor calling for Adam Rook please."

"Dr. Rook is busy at the moment."

"Tell him I need to speak with him urgently."

"Is this a medical emergency?"

"No it's personal. Get him on the phone now!"

Sensing a bit of anger in the caller's voice, the receptionist says "Just a moment sir."

After being placed on hold and listening to the recorded message about how compassionate Premier doctors are and then some elevator music, Adam Rook answered.

"Good morning Jack, how are you? I see the messenger was able to locate you alright. Trust there is no problem."

"Adam, I'll get right to the point. You and I need to meet ASAP!"

"Well my plate is pretty full this week…"

"No bullshit Adam I need to talk with you now!"

"Whoa. Slow down buddy, if it's that important how about coming over in say an hour around ten?"

"No, I want to meet someplace where we won't be seen."

"Well let's see. I have a couple of important meetings until about five. Meet you after that."

"Fine meet me at the Crooked Point boat ramp on the lake at six."

"I will see you then."

As soon as Jack hung up, Rook phoned Rose.

"Brent, Victor just phoned me. Said he wanted to meet ASAP. Sounded a bit agitated and maybe even afraid. I think he is starting to unravel. I thought he was emotionally strong enough to go through with this. I thought I could count on him. I'm to meet him at Crooked Point at six."

"Look you meet with the SOB. Keep him in line. If he rats on this deal it'll cost both of us plenty. I don't like to lose. Call me as soon as you meet with him."

*****

Victor got to the boat ramp early, sat in his car trying to listen to the radio. He got out of the car, sat on a log and threw some stones into the water. It was a crisp early spring day. The trees not yet budding. The sun was beginning to set on the horizon. The lake was nearly deserted, just a few fishermen out on the water. Soon he saw some headlights approaching and he recognized Rook's Lexus. Shortly the doctor got out his car and approached Jack.

"Jack what's this all about?"

"Adam, I can't continue, I can't go through with this. What I did was wrong and perhaps illegal. You know it Rose knows it and I know it. Here's the envelope and the money. Take it I feel like a Judas. I want out."

Rook looked at him sternly, pushed the envelope into Victor's pocket.

"Look you son of a bitch. This is yours. You took it

and knew damn well what you were getting into. You're in this as deep as the rest of us. You sold yourself out. I don't give a shit if you're having trouble sleeping at night. Take a god damn sleeping pill. You got any idea what might happen to both of us if I take this back to Rose. Hell the man hates losing a god damn football game, how do you think he'll take losing this? If you think you're gonna fink out and implicate the rest of us you got another thing coming. So keep the damn money. Blow it on a mink for your wife or let it ride at the craps table in French Lick. The fuckin' money is yours. What's done is done, live with it!"

"Adam, I can't"

"Look you know damn well the deal was a good deal for the hospital. So we skirted some ethical issues. What matters is we got the job done!"

Just then a fisherman was putting his Jon boat in the water. He recognized Rook and came over to the two men. He was far enough away as to not have heard much of the conversation. As soon as Rook and Victor spotted him approaching them they stopped arguing.

"Hey, Doc Rook. Jessie Farmer here. You probably don't member me but you patched my busted leg up about six months back. Musta done a good lob I'm walking. Good to see you again. Looks like you both too dressed up to do much fishin' huh. Well gotta get to dem Bass while they're still hungry.

65

Good to see you"

When the fisherman was out of hearing range Rook said, "Victor keep the god damn money and keep your fucking mouth shut!"

Jack had never seen Rook so violent. He was beginning to fear for his safety.

With that Rook got into the Lexus, raced the engine, peeled the tires and sped off up the ramp onto the highway and back to town.

The squealing of the tires could be heard on the lake and old Jessie Farmer said to himself "Damn that noise was so loud it mighta scared all the bass. Hope not." He put the spinner bait on and cast into the submersed timber.

Jack felt like shit. He violated all his principles and now was humiliated by Rook. All he wanted to do was punch the guy out but instead he sat in his car intimidated, scarred and his head bowed. He knew that he could not keep the money or use it for his personal gain. He knew that what he did was wrong and he could not profit from a wrong. Fortunately, the only people who knew about it were Rose and Rook and of course Gabriella. He knew none of the three would say anything. He was also very fearful of what Rook might do.

He started the car and headed south toward home.

When he got home Gabriella was waiting. "How did it go?"

"Not too good. Rook was pissed. To tell you the truth I was scared. The man went ballistic on me. I think if he had a gun I'd be floating face down in the lake right now. He threw the money back in my face. It's still in the trunk of the car."

"What are we gonna do. You and I know we can't keep it."

"I know that. On the way home I was thinking that since the money came from involvement with the hospital, I'm going to make a series of small and anonymous donations to the new community foundation. That way some needy people will benefit. And if we keep the amounts small no one will get suspicious."

"Fine. What do you think Rook will do now?"

"Don't know. I hope nothing."

Somehow the knowledge that he would not realize any gain from his deed eased his conscience. For the first time in a long while he felt at peace.

*****

Rook went back to his office. Sarah his secretary

was at her desk working on a term paper for her V160 class. "Oh good evening Dr. Rook. Didn't think you would return. Hope you don't mind my using the office computer for my class work."

"No go ahead."

"By the way how'd the meeting with Mr. Victor go?"

Rook did not answer but from his mannerism Sarah knew things did not go well. She wasn't sure what the problem was but she knew it wasn't good. She had never seen her boss so agitated and upset.

Rook slammed the door to his office, picked up the phone and called Rose.

Rose answered on the second ring and without so much as a hello or inquiring who was calling said "How'd the meeting go?"

"Not too good. As we suspected Victor wanted out and tried to return the money. I told him in plain English that he was in this up to his ears and the money was his and no way in hell was he going to implicate anyone else. I just left him at the lake. Hell the guy is a basket case"

"Son of a bitch! I knew we couldn't trust that little bastard; he didn't have big enough balls to go through with it. I warned you about him- ah shit. If he finks out and leaks this to the press or even to the hospital we both are in deep shit. If this deal falls through we both figure to lose a shit full of money, not to say worse. You know the syndicate up north is chomping at the bit to buy the hospital from us. If we flip this deal we're sitting pretty. Look this is your problem you do whatever it takes to make sure that little shit keeps his mouth shut; and I mean whatever it takes. You understand me? Take care of it!"

"What do you mean 'Take care of it'?"

"Take care of it.! Do whatever it takes to keep his mouth shut. We have too much at stake to let that bastard ruin us. Everything we worked for our lives, reputation resources are all on the line. Keep him quiet and do whatever it takes. You understand?"

"Yes"

*****

The next two days were much better for Jack. He stopped his excessive drinking. He went back to productivity at work finishing his article on the economic impact of universal health coverage. The thought that the money would be given to provide care for the indigent eased his conscience. He rationalized that he would not realize any financial gain personally from the money and the community would have a nice sized trust fund to pay for indigent care. He and Gabriella resumed talking about taking the summer trip to Italy that they had been planning and saving for. For the first time in a long while Jack felt good about himself. He called home.

"Gabriella, I'm gonna be home a little bit late. I have a bunch of stuff here to finish up. I'm getting a lot done I'll probably be home in about two hours."

"OK Jack, I'm a bit behind on dinner. Got home late from school, Mrs. Smithfield came to see me about Brian so we'll have a late dinner. See you then be careful. Love you."

"I love you too, why don't you call the playhouse and see if you get two good seats for Saturday night."

"Will do, bye."

Jack hung up the phone. It was already dark when he left the building. The parking lot was empty with the exception of one black Mitsubishi Eclipse in the corner of the lot. Jack looked at the car. He liked the styling and performance of that car and was seriously thinking about replacing his Sebring convertible with one. Campus was unusually quiet, perhaps because the Cougars were playing an important basketball game in Ann Arbor for first place in the conference. It was also the start of Spring break and many students had left earlier for warmer climates. Those who remained were at the bars watching big screen T.V. The quietness was something Jack desperately needed. As he started his car and started to pull out of the lot he thought about that black Eclipse.

"Yea, maybe that's what I should get when the lease on the Sebring expires. Black exterior with black leather bucket seats and maybe we'll go for the manual transmission. Should I get the coupe or the convertible? I'll let Gabriella decide. If she gets pregnant as we hope this may be the last fun car I can have. I wonder how I will like driving a minvan. Maybe I'll call Tom at Curry's and see what deals he's got. I can also see Jay at Town and Country and see what deals he has on a new convertible. It'll be fun to shop for a new set of wheels."

As he exited the lot and headed south he noticed that the black Eclipse was also leaving and going south. He headed down 73 making a left on Lake Road and headed home. He kept noticing the black Eclipse following him. As he got on Lake Road he sensed the space between he and the Eclipse was getting shorter. "What's with that guy? He's almost on my bumper."

As they started down the eight mile stretch of a winding and hilly road, the Eclipse kept getting closer and closer. Jack slowed down and got over on to the right shoulder hoping the car would pass. As they passed the row of new condominiums he glanced into the rearview mirror. "What the hell is that son of a bitch following me?" He wondered. He noticed that the Eclipse was speeding up and getting closer and closer to his rear bumper. Just then he felt a jolt. "Oh what the hell was that? Damn he just hit me" And then another harder bump. "What's with that crazy bastard?" Jack decided to slow down and let the car pass. As he did the two cars came side by side traveling down the narrow road. Jack tried to accelerate but as he did the Eclipse accelerated even more. And then a sudden scraping sound as the two fenders met. The Eclipse's front end turned right and began pushing Jack's car off the road.

Both drivers lost control and the two vehicles began to tumble down the steep ravine rolling over and over end for end. The sounds of fallen leaves were crunching beneath the cars. Jack's Sebring rolls over crushing the soft rag top. The Eclipse manages to stay on its wheels and comes to a stop crashing into a large Sycamore tree. The wheels of the upside down Sebring were still spinning creating an eerie sound in the otherwise silent eve.

Jack stayed motionless, unconscious. The driver of the other car tried to move but could not.

*****

Jim Merit a neighbor of the Victors was taking a leisurely drive home listening to the Cougars take a ten point lead and feeling pretty good about his taking the Cougars minus six. The skid marks in the pavement caught his attention. "Gee I know these were not here when I came down the road. Something must have happened recently." He slowed to see if he could tell what happened. The tires in the fallen leaves left their mark. Jim's eyes followed them and he thought he spotted the glow of headlights in the ravine below. Stopping he got out of his car and saw the two vehicles. He called 911 and reported the accident.

About 20 minutes later a sheriff's deputy arrived on the scene and called for backup, ambulances and tow vehicles.

"Is he dead?"

"No but damn near."

Paramedics used the Jaws of Life to remove the driver of the Eclipse. Jack was still unconscious when the paramedics placed him on the gurney and into the ambulance. The medics arrived at Midland General in about fifteen minutes both men were rushed to the E.R

*****

Gabriella was in a pleasant mood. Fixing some pasta with clam sauce and listening to the Three Tenors' CD when her solitude was interrupted by the ring of the telephone.

"Mrs. Victor?"

"Yes"

"This is Gloria Page I am a nurse with the Midland E.R. I'm afraid your husband has been in an accident. The ambulance transported him about 15 minutes ago."

"No no it can't be. Is he alright?"

"All I know at this time is the injuries are serious."

"I'm on my way."

It took her about 25 minutes to get to the hospital. Heading straight for the ER she was greeted by a receptionist and escorted to exam room two.

"Mrs. Victor, I'm Dr. Jensen. Your husband has been seriously injured and is in surgery."

"How bad?"

"Right now we do not know the full extent. He suffered massive internal bleeding and severe damage to the spinal cord. He is in surgery now. I'll keep you posted. Sorry but I need to tend to the other patient."

Gabriella sat in the waiting room outside of the operating suite for what seemed like an eternity. About two hours later a nurse reported that Jack was now out of surgery but has not fully recovered and would be taken to the ICU. She would able to see him shortly.

She stayed at the hospital through out the night. Around 6:30 she was awakened by Dr. Hicks who discussed Jack's condition with her. He told her that Jack's injuries were extremely severe and that the next 48 hours would be critical. In other such injuries he treated, the patient generally regained full mental capacity.

However, right now he did not think Jack would recover the use of his legs. The injuries to the spinal cord were so massive that they resulted in paralysis to his lower body. She was told that there was not much more she could do now and it would be sometime before Jack awoke.

"Mrs. Victor, go home, get some rest and come back in the afternoon."

"I really can't. I need to stay with my husband."

"I think it would be in the best interest of all that you get some rest. When he comes to he will need your support."

Reluctantly she left went home took a long hot shower and fell asleep.

*****

Billie Franklin the driver of the black Eclipse was taken to Midland and admitted to room 413.

His injuries were not life threatening, a few broken ribs and a broken left femur. Apparently the airbags in the Eclipse did their job. He was resting comfortably. The only visitor he had was Naomi Hoag.

Chapter 5
The Turning Point

Rook stood in his bathroom preparing to head for the hospital. He hadn't slept well last night. Rose's words "Do whatever it takes" ringing in his ears. What did Rose mean by the words "whatever it takes"? The emphatic way he said "whatever" gave Rook some cause for alarm. Would Victor be so stupid and so weak as to spill the beans? What if he deposited the money in one large sum? How would such a large deposit be explained? How do we keep him quiet? What do we do if he talks?

"I need to get back into the ER see some patients and clear my head of this mess"

He was on his way to the hospital when he heard the news report "Early last evening Professor Jack Victor was seriously injured in a two car accident on Lake Road south of town. The professor is currently in intensive care at Midland General. University officials have no further information." What, Rook thought to himself. Could he have been so lucky that fate took care of the matter?

When he arrived at the hospital Jim Pleasant was on duty.

Rook was glad to see his colleague "Morning Jim you on duty, it's been awhile since we worked together."

"Yea pulled a double shift. Minor asked me to fill in for him. I'm damn tired too. Say I haven't seen you working the ER for awhile. What, all that high powered administration stuff get to you?"

"Yea, Olivia asked me to take her shift. Feels good to be able to see paitents again. All that book keeping stuff, the mess with Premier buying the hospital. It all makes me long to get my hands messy in the E. R again."

"Good to have you in the trenches. Sure was a busy night last night. Did you hear about the accident on Lake Road?"

"I heard it on the news as I was driving in."

"Yea, a real bad crash. From what I heard, seems some college kid ran him off the road. The kid is in 413 don't think his injuries are as severe. Victor suffered massive spinal cord damage. May never walk again. Sure hope he recovers enough to keep teaching."

"Hm too bad he's a nice guy." What Rook wanted to say was that he hoped he'd never be able to talk again.

"OK Adam have a good shift. Shouldn't be too busy the Cougars are on the road. One more victory and we got the conference title again and that all important first round tournament bye."

"Yea, take care. And get some rest."

*****

Gabriella spent all of the second day at the hospital next to Jack who lied motionless in the ICU. The nurses convinced her that it would be best for all if she left and spent the night at home and got some needed rest.

"I'll call you if there is any change."

"Thank you."

She drove back to the lake house. As she turned onto Lake Road and the row of condominiums and the now infamous ravine her heart began to pound, her legs tightened and her palms began to sweat. She could not bear to look at the site but instead kept her eyes focused straight ahead. She pulled into the garage and headed straight for the bedroom fell on the bed and crashed. She awoke about five-thirty, showered dressed and ate a small bowl of Granola. She glanced through the local paper and then took a short walk down to the lake. She stood at the shoreline looking at the new sunrise and her thoughts were of Jack and how he loved being on the lake. They had been shopping for a small cuddy cabin and almost put a down payment on a twenty foot Bayliner. She convinced Jack that perhaps they should think about the deal for a week and talk about it. They planned on returning to the dealer with a check on Saturday. She thought how excited he would be launching his first boat- the captain of the fleet. Now all of that is gone. Now the best she could hope for was that he would be alive. She stood there and cried. Oh she loved him so much, why did God allow this to happen?

*****

When Gabriella arrived at the hospital she learned that Jack had been moved from intensive care to the general medical surgical wing and is now in room 415. She took the elevator to the fourth floor and as she passed the nurses station she was greeted by Dr. Hicks.

"Oh, good morning Mrs. Victor. Last night we moved your husband out of intensive care and into room 415. He is progressing rather nicely."

"Thank you doctor. May I see him now?"

"Of course."

She entered his room to see him still hooked up to tubes and not awake. She gave him a kiss and told him how much she loved him then took her seat next to the bed. She stayed at the bedside the entire day leaving his side to only get a bite to eat and talk with the nurses. Gary called a couple of times to see how Jack was doing and came to visit after lunch. Around 8:00 she left the hospital and went home. Once again as soon as she turned onto Lake Road her body began to tense. Her legs began to tighten and this horrible feeling came over. She wondered if she would ever be able to travel that stretch of road feeling at ease.

She got home, checked the mail, nothing too important. The answering machine was full of messages; colleagues from the university calling to see how Jack was doing, Jack's sister and of course the courtesy call from Shell Oil.

She put some water in a pot to prepare some pasta, opened a bottle of Bolla Merlot and called Jack's sister. She was not on the phone long. Just long enough to give Beth an update on Jack's condition and tell her she would call later in the week after she got some rest and knew more about the future and that there was no need for Beth to fly in from Philadelphia at this time.

After dinner she went upstairs took a long hot bath in the whirlpool tub, got into bed and continued reading the latest Patricia Cornwell novel she started at the hospital. She did not get a good's night sleep and got out of bed at six. She showered quickly, ate a small bowl of granola and two cups of coffee and left for the hospital. As she passed the row of condominiums she again began to cry.

*****

She entered the room and saw Jack as she saw him the previous day. An I.V tube providing nourishment and medication, heart monitoring and other wires attached to his body monitoring his vitals. She went to the bed leaned over squeezed his hand and kissed him and whispered "I love you" and took a seat next to the bed. The silence in the room was only interrupted by the beeping of the monitors.

Gabriella went to the hospital cafeteria for a light lunch. She passed over the pies and entrees and settled for a chicken salad, bottle water and an orange. She found a small table near the doctor's dinning room and sat and ate her meal. A tap on the shoulder and she heard a familiar voice of Marc Derrick. Marc was the hospital vice president for professional services. Gabriella met Marc and Helen Derrick when she had their son Damon in her third grade. They worked on PTA projects together.

"Good afternoon Gabriella."

"Oh, hi Marc"

"I'm so sorry about Jack's accident, what a terrible thing to have happened. How's he doing?"

"Marc thanks for asking, he came out of the surgery alright and is now in room 415. He is still unconscious but stable. The doctors are not sure if he will regain the use of his legs though."

"I'm so sorry to hear that. Our prayers are for you and your husband. If there is anything you need please do not hesitate to call me. I know that the entire administration team is worried and concerned for his recovery. You tell him we are praying for him."

"How is Damon doing in high school?"

"He's doing very well, must have been that St. Matthew's training. He is running track"

"Wonderful, he's a great kid he'll do o.k. Tell Helen I said hello."

"Will do, and remember to let me know if there is something you need, bye"

"Bye Marc and thanks."

Gabriella deposited her plastic eating utensils in the trash can and headed back to the fourth floor. Jack's condition had not changed. About an hour later she got up and walked around the room looking at Jack she began to see his eyes slowly open, they seemed to follow her. He tried to speak but his voice too weak to be heard. She leaned over the bed kissed him and cried but this time tears of joy. Throughout that afternoon he made slow but steady progress and by dinner time was able to speak in a low voice and move his arms.

Dr. Hicks examined Jack in the evening. He told Gabriella that it would be best if she went home and both of them got some rest. Outside the room he gave her a more complete report.

"The progress your husband made today is very encouraging. I think he is out of the woods but I am still not pleased with his lack of feeling in the lower extremities. I'm afraid that your husband will never walk again. I'm sorry to have to tell you that but the prognosis is not good."

"Thank you doctor, at least I will have my husband."

She left the hospital at 6:15 as she passed the nurses' station Donna Perkins bid her a good night.

*****

For the first time in days she felt relaxed. She interpreted Dr. Hicks' words as encouraging. She was beginning to come to grips with the fact that Jack may never be able to walk again. She called Beth to tell her the good news and they talked for fifteen minutes. As she hung up the telephone Gary called.

She told him about Jack's recovering and how excited she was.

"Gary I know it was just a small step forward and that he still can't walk but I'm so happy tonight. For the first time in days I know that I will have my husband back. Things will be different from what we planned but we may still see our golden anniversary."

"That's wonderful Gabby. I'm so happy for you and Jack. I'll stop by the hospital for a very short visit on my way home from the paper."

As he hung up the phone Gary could not help but have a sense of mixed emotions. He was on one hand pleased that his long time friend would still be alive. But another side of him kept telling him that this meant, of course, that he would not be able to share his love for Gabby. Once again he was to be the groomsman never the groom. And then he thought the unthinkable- maybe if Jack had died he could then be with Gabby.

*****

Gabby hung up the phone and sat quietly for awhile. She rationalized that while Jack might never walk again; at least he will be alive. Though things would be quite different they will still be together. Maybe they can still take the Italy trip. She thought about how the house would need to be remodeled to accommodate a wheelchair. Maybe we can build a new master bedroom suite on the first floor. She got a sheet of paper and began to sketch out how an office and bedroom suite could be added to the first floor. She left the paper on the kitchen table and went upstairs. She kept thinking about how great it was to see Jack able to look at her and how nice it would be to once again feel his warm body next to hers at night. With those thoughts in mind she fell fast asleep even though it was only ten o'clock.

*****

Dr. Rook entered the E.R around 6:00 p.m. Jim Pleasant was once again on duty and greeted Rook, "You here again Adam. Boy two nights in a row. You must really be bothered by that administration stuff."

"Right. Olivia's son has the flu or something so I volunteered to take her late shift."

"Oh, I didn't know Olivia was on the schedule. I thought she had a few days off, I thought Ownes was to relieve me. Have a quiet night. Things have been unusually slow, hope it stays that way for you. See ya."

"OK have a good night."

Things in the ER were slow. Rook took the opportunity to check on the status of a patient, Jack Victor.

"Damn, he's recovering. I still have this fear that he is going to rat on us." He said to himself.

*****

Meanwhile on the fourth floor Naomi Hoag was making a visit to room 415. She entered the room, closed the door behind her and stayed about 15 minutes. On the way out she met Dr. Rook.

"Good evening Dr. Rook. What brings you up here?"

Fumbling for words he says "Oh, I just wanted to see how our esteemed Board President is doing."

"Yes, Dr. Rook we are all praying for his speedy recovery."

"Yes, let us all pray." But thinking to himself Rook added "for a speedy death."

"Good night."

"Good night."

Rook entered the room and he too closed the door behind him. He was in the room for about ten minutes. As he left, he didn't turn right to go past the nurse's station to take an elevator down to the E.R. but instead turned left went down the back steps to the lower level, walked past the lockers out the doctor's entrance to the doctor's parking lot got in his car and headed home. Dr. Ownes will be working the E.R. as Dr. Olivia had originally scheduled.

*****

Shortly before midnight Gabriella was awakened by the ringing of the telephone.

"Hello"

"Mrs. Victor?"

"Yes"

"This is Donna Perkins; I am a nurse at Midland. I'm very sorry to tell you this but your husband suffered a massive heart attack. The doctors did…"

"Is he, is he… alright?"

"The doctors did all they could…"

"No no it can't be."

"I'm very sorry."

After a long pause Gabriella told the nurse she would leave for the hospital immediately.

She dressed quickly got into her car sped down Lake Road. However, this time she was going so fast and her mind thinking about Jack that she did not even see the fatal ravine. She arrived at the hospital and not wanting to wait for an elevator quickly took the stairs to the fourth floor. Upon entering the room she saw Jack's body lying still in the bed. The nurse had already removed all of the monitoring and I.V tubes. He looked at peace. She went to his bedside and kissed his forehead and cheek and began to cry. She stood at the bedside motionless as if in a catatonic state. Nurse Perkins entered the room and put her arm around Gabriella, hugged her and told her how sorry all of the staff was about Jack's death.

"Stay as long as you like, Mrs. Victor. We will need to know the name of the funeral home you want to take care of Mr. Victor."

Gabriella stood there for a moment not responding. Nurse Perkins again asked her for the name of the funeral home. Gabriella thought for a moment.

"I'm not sure."

She and Jack had not discussed final arrangements. She did recall that when his father died Jack was very happy with the services of Fry and Fry. Without thinking further she said.

"Fry and Fry on Rogers Street. Yes please call Fry."

"OK. Is there anything I can get for you? Maybe some coffee or a soda?"

"No I'm fine."

With that nurse Perkins left the room and called Fry and Fry.

About an hour later two middle aged gentlemen dressed in dark suits and dark ties entered the room.

"Mrs. Victor I'm Jacob Fry and this is my brother Joshua. We are so sorry for the loss. We will do whatever we can to make this very sad time bearable for you. Please do not hesitate to let us know if there is anything we can do."

"Thank you."

"Whenever you are ready we will transport Mr. Victor."

Gabriella leaned over to Jack and whispered something in his ear. She held his hand tightly and gave him one last kiss. After a moment she turned to Jacob Fry and merely nodded.

"It might be best if you waited outside."

Nurse Perkins took Gabriella into the hallway as the two men lifted Jack's body onto a gurney into the body bag and zipped up the side. They then wheeled the gurney into the hallway down a corridor to the service elevator. Gabriella followed. The men and gurney got into the elevator with Gabriella and pushed the basement button. The elevator slowly descended the five levels to the basement area. Fry and his brother pushed the gurney past linen carts out the delivery entrance and into the waiting hearse. Gabriella waited until the door of the hearse closed. Joshua Fry asked her to come to the parlor the next morning to make arrangements for the visitation and burial. Gabriella only nodded. When the hearse was out of sight; she walked around the building to parking lot 3, got into the car and started home, this time very slowly.

As she turned onto Lake Road she began to tense. Once again her legs felt taut her heart beat faster and her stomach turned. She stopped at the crash site got out of the car and stared down the step ravine. She sobbed. Then in a loud voice-

"Why? Why God did you let this happen? There was no good reason for his death? Why, why, why? Bring him back!"

After a few minutes she got back into the car and continued home. She parked the car outside, opened the front door and went straight upstairs. Without changing clothes she laid on the bed still asking why oh why did this happen.

She did not get much sleep. Only dosing off for 20-30 minutes then waking up and reaching over to Jack's side of the bed, hoping that maybe just maybe she would once again feel the warmth of his body. Of course this was not to happen.

She finally got out of bed about 6:30 went into the bathroom and saw Jack's white terry cloth robe hanging on the hook next to the shower. She reached for her toothbrush and instead picked up Jack's. She looked at the brush and began to cry.

In the kitchen she only felt like a glass of orange juice and a couple cups of coffee. She slowly drank the coffee in the quiet of the kitchen; on the table was the sketch she made for the room addition. Finishing the coffee she went upstairs. In the bedroom she stood before Jack's closet. She thought she remembered one of the Fry brothers telling her to bring his final clothes to the home, but most of last night was a blur in her memory. She selected his navy suit with the faint pinstripe. He said that wearing that suit made him feel comfortable. It was the one he wore for special occasions and when he was giving an important speech. She picked out a blue gray diamond pattern tie, white on white dress shirt and black socks and shoes. She put the outfit into his hanging bag, got dressed and headed for the funeral parlor.

Once again she had to pass the fatal ravine. This time she did not look to the side of the road but instead focused on the road ahead, her eyes swelled with tears now rolling down her cheeks.

*****

She got to Fry and Fry around nine. Both brothers were already at work and greeted her at the entrance. Again they expressed their condolences and explained that she would need to select the casket and tell them her plans on the time of the visitation, and the burial arrangements. The younger Fry brother escorted her into the showroom where the walls were lined with various caskets. On the left wall were the female caskets and on the right wall the male caskets; not that it made much difference she thought. She selected a mid price range wooden casket. Jack always said people should be buried in a wooden not metal box.

"Ah the Batesville Mediterranean Oak- Excellent choice it is one of our more popular models. Mrs. Victor; now if you will please follow me we can make the other arrangements and prepare his obituary."

Even though both men tried very hard to be compassionate; Gabriella thought the process so far was cold. It seemed to her that they were mostly interested in the business end and trying to softly sell her the most expensive "package".

"Please have a seat. May I get you something perhaps a coffee or latté?"

"No thank you."

Joshua Fry began to ask her for her preferences; time of visitation, where the body would be laid to rest, other related matters and of course gave her the price list for various services.

They agreed that visitation would be the day after

next from four to nine p.m. The Mass of Resurrection would be held at St. Matthew's the following morning at ten and then burial at Memorial Gardens. Mr. Fry then called St. Matthews to verify that Mass on Thursday could be scheduled. Ann answered the phone.

"St. Matthews Parish"

"Good morning Ann this is Adam Fry, how are you today?

"Fine"

"Mrs. Victor is in my office and we were wondering if ten on Thursday would be a good time to have the funeral Mass?"

"Let me check the calendar. Yes ten is open, would you like me to see if Fr, Charlie is available to officiate?"

"Yes would you please?"

"OK. He is at home but I will call him and then let you know right away. Tell Mrs. Victor that we are all so sorry to have heard of her loss and will be praying for her."

Fry hung up the phone and the two went over other details and wrote the obituary. About ten minutes later the telephone rang.
"Mr. Fry, Ann here. Fr. Charlie said it would be his

honor to officiate the Mass for Jack and the time is ok with him. He hopes you will express his condolences to Gabriella. You know Jack was very active in our parish. Fr. Charlie will try and stop by their house."

"Fine then. Everything is set on your end." With that he hung up the phone.

A half hour later Gabrielle was on her way home. It would be a long afternoon and night one of many more to come. She checked the mail and placed the envelopes on the dining room table. She then called Beth to give her the funeral details. Beth said she would book a flight as soon as possible and be in Midland soon. Both women then cried.

*****

The next morning the *Herald* ran a long article in the local deaths section of the paper. **"UNIVERSITY PROFESSOR DIES FROM COMPLICATIONS OF AUTO CRASH"** read the headline of the article. It contained quotes from Jack's dean on how valuable he was to the program. Students talked about what an inspiration he was and how he helped them in their careers. City officials talked about his service to the community. Dr. Rose was quoted as saying what a great leader and man of vision he was. Of course Naomi Hoag added her condolences and said what a good board president he was having led the board through some difficult times; the hiring of a CEO for the first time in

19 years, the implementation of a cardiac care and rehabilitation unit and of course, the selling to Premier. Rook offered no comments. Gabriella read the quotes by Rose and Hoag a couple of times but somehow she did not think the two were sincere.

She did not get much sleep. On the day of the funeral she finally got out of bed around four thirty. She put a load of dirty clothes in the washer, and brewed a pot of coffee. As she passed the kitchen table she saw the paper on which she had sketched the first floor wheelchair accessible master bedroom suite she had planned for Jack's return. Only a few days ago she was planning an addition to the first floor to accommodate a wheelchair confined husband. Today she was planning to attend his funeral. She just stared at the sketch, then crumpled the paper threw it across the room and shouted "Why? Why? Why? Why did God let this happen?"

At two o'clock she dressed got into her car for the drive to the funeral home. Before she backed out of the garage she sat thinking about having to drive past the ravine. She thought that after a few days the passage would be easier but each time it seemed to be more difficult.

*****

She arrived at the funeral home and met Beth. Jacob Fry escorted Gabriella into Parlor A for some private moments with her husband before the crowd arrived. The room was filled with floral pieces. Of course there was a large bouquet from the School, another large piece in which the card simply said "From your students. You will be missed. Go in Peace." There were also twenty yellow roses from the Premier Group.

Shortly before four the first group of mourners arrived. By five o'clock the line was backed up into the parking lot with about a twenty minute wait. The flow of mourners was fairly constant until about eight thirty. With no one waiting in the queue Gabriella had her first chance to sit down. Gary sat next to her drying the tears that were running down her cheek.

"Gary I don't know what I am going to do without Jack. I don't know if I can cope with such a loss. We never talked about our own deaths; we just assumed that we would be married into our golden years. You know we were planning a trip to Italy this summer."

"I know Gabby. No one can feel your hurt. But you are a strong woman- you will get through this. You know I will always be here to help you. If ever you need anything just call me. OK?"

"Gary you're a good friend. I am not sure what I would do without your support."

It was nine fifteen and Gary said he should be getting home, besides the Fry brothers wanted to close up and leave.

"See you tomorrow Gabby"

"Thank you Gary. Good night, see you tomorrow. Thank you for everything."

She gave him a kiss on the check, he hugged her and they both left.

*****

It was another lonely night for Gabriella. She finally dozed off to sleep about three thirty at six thirty the alarm went off.

"Good morning it's six thirty and you're listening to your favorite music on 102.8 FM. Today in Midland should be gorgeous. Sunny with a high temperature of…"

Gabriella could not listen to much of Ms Sunshine today. Usually she got a chuckle out of the radio personality, but today was not a time for laughter. She went to the kitchen poured her orange juice and coffee and sat quietly. Somehow she had no desire for her usual breakfast of granola and a ripe banana. Jack had teased her about eating so much granola and how could she eat the same breakfast everyday. Jack was a large eggs, bacon toast or hotcakes, or French toast kind of breakfast guy.

She finished her coffee went upstairs to get dressed. Once again she had to face the dreaded drive past the ravine.

When she arrived at the funeral home a small crowd of mourners was already there. The Fry brothers had opened the parlor and a group had gathered around the casket. When they saw Gabriella enter they parted and made a pathway for her to Jack's side.

At nine o'clock Adam Fry announced that it was close to the time they had to depart for St. Matthews and asked that mourners who would like to pay their last respect please do so. One by one they came to the casket and then exited to the foyer. Gary and Gabriella stood there alone in the quiet. Gary knelt down and said a short prayer then touched Jack's shoulder.

"Good bye old friend. I know you are now at peace."

He left to wait with the others in the foyer.

Gabriella leaned over the casket and gave Jack a kiss.

"Good bye my love. I will never stop loving you. Wait for me."

She then left the parlor and the two Fry brothers closed the parlor doors, removed the pillow from beneath Jack's head, closed the casket lid and locked the top shut. They then asked the pall bearers to come in and assist with taking the casket to the waiting hearse.

The ride to St. Matthews was a short one. As they pulled into the circular drive in front of the church Ed had the bells ringing. Fr. Charlie was waiting in his white vestments, and greeted Gabriella. As the casket entered the sanctuary, Father asked the family- Gabriella and Jack's sister along with Gary to place the white pall on the casket. He sprinkled the casket with holy water said a prayer and led the procession into the front of the church at the foot of the main altar.

Seated to the right of the altar was Gabriella's class. Father then began the Mass. He offered a nice, but bit long, homily bringing in some humor. He mentioned how when he came to St. Matthew's five years ago Jack was one of the first parishioners to welcome him, taking him to lunch at Big Daddy's.

After the mass the procession left for Memorial Gardens. When they arrived at the site the pall bearers carried the casket to the grave. Father blessed the ground and the casket once more. Said an Our Father, Hail Mary and Glory Be. One by one the mourners came up and placed a red rose on the casket.

Adam Fry said "This concludes our services. Mrs. Victor would like to invite all of you back to the social hall at St. Matthews for a light lunch."

*****

The We Care group had a couple of tables nicely

decorated with cheese trays, meat trays and fruit and desserts on a long banquet table. About 40 people came back for the lunch. Around two-thirty they began to leave once again expressing condolences to Gabriella. By three-twenty only Gary and Gabriella remained.

"Gary could you come to our place when we leave here? I would like some company."

"Sure I'll follow you out."

Chapter 6
The Hunch

Gabriella and Gary entered the house through the garage and sat in the family room.

"Would you like a glass of wine? I have a bottle of merlot open from the other night.

"Love to, thanks."

As they sipped on the wine Gabriella looked at Gary, paused and then said

"Gary, I have something I want to share with you. But I need to share this with Gary Riggs longtime friend not Gary Riggs reporter. Alright"

"Sure"

"You must give me your word that everything I'm about to tell you is strictly off the record. I'm counting on you as a long time friend of Jack and me. Can I feel confident that you will not publish this?"

"Gabby, you know I think the world of you and your friendship means more to me than any byline. You sound worried."

"OK"

She then went on to tell him about the bribe and the money and how they gave it all to the Community Foundation.

"Gary, I don't think Jack died of natural causes. Call it women's intuition, a wife's hysteria or even just irrationality but I think Jack was murdered. I had an autopsy performed on his remains. Complete- organ analysis, blood analysis the works. Dr. Hicks told me he was progressing nicely. He was in excellent health I don't know what happened but I am convinced he did not die from injuries sustained in that crash or a heart attack."

"You got any results? Any proof to support what you claim?"

"The results of the autopsy are not ready yet. But Jack met with Rook and tried to give him the money back. Rook got very angry and said that if anyone found out about the 'consulting fee' as Rook called the money Jack would have serious regrets. When

103

Jack came home he was scared. Even shaking a bit he told me he feared for his life at the lake meeting and didn't know what Rook was capable of. I'd never seen him so frightened; not even when we encountered that black bear in the Smokies. I don't know what or how but something was done to him."

"Gabby, what you're saying is serious. We just can't…"

"I know Gary, that's why I'm telling you all this. Hoping that you can help me get some proof."

"OK. Look I know Mike Huest one of the homicide detectives with the police department. Mike owes me a couple of favors for not going public with a few officer misconducts. I'll call him in the morning."

"Thanks Gary, I knew you would help."

"No problem."

Gabriella told him all she knew about the meeting with Rook and the fear in Jack's voice when he came home and told her what had happened. She then placed a Tony Bennett CD on and they listened silently. They finished the bottle of merlot and sat together on the couch as Gary listened to the romantic ballads he could not stop thinking about how much he still loved Gabriella and how he so much wanted to take her in his arms and kiss her passionately. But one more time out of his respect and love for his friend Jack he resisted. As Tony Bennett finished his rendition of "As Time Goes By" Gabriella turned slowly and held his hand. She looked deeply into his eyes and asked "Gary, one other thing- can you stay tonight? I can prepare the guest room I think I need the comfort of having someone in the house tonight"

"Of course."

Gabriella went upstairs and prepared the guest room and set out a fresh set of towels. It would be nice having a man in the house again.

"Well I better get to bed. It's late I am going to go to school tomorrow. Might as well get back to teaching. Maybe work will ease the grief."

"I think that's a good idea. Good night."

Gary went to bed and stared at the ceiling knowing that he and the woman he loved were separated by five inches. He so much wanted to go to her room take her in his arms and make passionate love. He never got over the love he had for her, but was too good a friend of Jack's to let his true feelings be known. Maybe now that Jack's dead, but when or how? He knew tonight was not the time. The last thing he ever wanted to do was hurt Gabriella. He loved her too much to do that. But he also knew that it was an unrequited love. She was still deeply in love with Jack.

Early next morning he heard Gabriella in the kitchen. He quickly dressed and went downstairs. Gabriella had made him a breakfast of hotcakes and sausages and had a fresh pot of coffee brewed.

"Good morning Gary, hope you slept well."

"Yea like a log." Of course this was a lie but he could not tell her that his longing for her kept him awake and restless most of the night.

"Good you want some orange juice?"

"No thanks the coffee will be fine. Everything smells good"

"Eat up."

She poured herself a large glass of juice, a cup of coffee and bowl of granola. Gabriella was coming back to her old self. When she finished she said she needed to head off to St. Matthews, she didn't want to be late on the first day back. She gave Gary a quick kiss on the cheek and thanked him for staying the night. His presence in the next room gave her comfort.

Sure like he needed to be thanked for staying. He so much wanted to take her in his arms and tell her how he felt; but once again his loyalty to a dead friend blocked him. He cleaned up the kitchen, got into his car and left. On the drive to the office his thoughts were with Gabriella and how much he wanted to spend the rest of his life with her. He thought Jack the lucky one for having at least six years with her, at this point in time he would gladly change places with his friend.

After checking his e-mail he picked up the phone and called the Midland Police Department.

"Hello Midland Police"

"Good morning, this is Gary Riggs calling for Lt. Mike Huest."

A few moments later the detective answers the phone.

"Gary good day to you. You calling to see if we want to tee off later this afternoon?"

"No I have to work to earn money so I can pay off my golf debts. By the way if you ever repeat that coughing as I am putting for a birdie I'm…"

"Hey hold on old buddy. You know I have allergies. It was the pollen that made me cough not the even round."

"Yea yea. Mike seriously, I need to talk to you about something that may be a police matter."

"Sure, what's on your mind?"

"I can't talk over the phone. Can you meet me for a late lunch; say one o'clock at the Jib Room on the east end of the lake?"

"Sure, that's the place with the good catfish sandwich. I'll be there."

"Thanks see you."

Mike did not think much of the call. Surely if it involved Gary he could not be in any serious trouble. Gary never had so much as a speeding ticket.

Gary finished his article on the million dollar water spillway the mayor is proposing as a gateway to the city. He answered some e-mails and then headed to the Jib Room. Both men got to the restaurant's parking lot about the same time. They entered the restaurant and sat at a booth at the back of the lounge. The Jib Room was nearly empty. Because of its location it does not do a good lunch crowd on week days. Friday night is catfish night. All the fried catfish you can eat plus a live Bluegrass band. The place is packed with standing room only for the entertainment.

Shortly a young waitress comes to the table.

"Good afternoon gentleman, my name is Terri and I'll be happy to serve you gentlemen today. Can I get you something from the bar?"

"I'll have a Michelob Amber draft."

"Me too."

When the beers came both ordered a large pork tenderloin sandwich with the works. Gary had fried onion rings and Mike ordered the French fries. During lunch they talked about golf and the Cougars. When they finished Gary got to the point of the meeting.

"Mike, you know the university professor, Jack Victor, who died from injuries in a car crash on Lake Road."

"Yea I read about it, didn't know him; so?"

"I have some reasons to believe that the injuries did not kill him but rather he was murdered. I think someone gave him a dose of a chemical that mimics a heart attack. Right now I don't have more than a hunch. But the pathologist's autopsy report should be ready in a few days. I would like you to take a look at the report and give me your expert opinion."

"Sure, have'em send me a copy and I'll take a look."

"Thanks Mike,"

Both men finished eating and Gary went to pick up both checks.

"Nope, got to pay for my own lunch. Don't want the Internal Affairs people to think I took a bribe."

"Sure, that's all you're worth any way- a sandwich and a beer."

Both men laughed got up and left the room.

"We still on for an eight o'clock tee time on Saturday?"

"Yep, see you then bye Mike and thanks again for looking into this."

*****

When Gary got back to the *Herald* he called Gabriella who was just getting home from class. He told her about the meeting with Mike Huest and asked her to call the pathologist's office and ask them to send a copy of the report to Mike. He asked how her first day back had gone. She said she was glad to hear that someone would look into Jack's death. Said the day went well and she was looking forward to getting back into action. After thanking him they both hung up the phone.

The weekend went quietly for Gabriella. She spent most of the time walking in the woods around the property and reminiscing about her years with Jack. Even though she enjoyed her walks the weekend seemed extraordinarily long. She realized how lonely and empty her life would now be without Jack. She sat on the deck looked out at the row of Sycamores and wept.

*****

On Tuesday a messenger delivered a package to Lt. Mike Huest. He read it and noted the finding "Cause of death- massive cardiac infarction." Interesting. Seems Gary was wrong. His friend died of natural causes. He put the file aside and continued to work leads on the 14th street burglary.

Gabriella arrived home on Tuesday evening to see the medical examiner's report in the stack of mail. She quickly tore open the envelope and began to read the details. No trace of above normal levels of chemicals found in tissue or fluids other than an elevated level of potassium in the blood, no evidence of trauma other than that sustained in the original crash and finally the cause of death myocardial infarction. "A heart attack" she cried but how? Jack was at a low risk for a heart attack, his last physical examination found him to be in excellent health. How could a relatively young man in good shape and physical condition die from a heart attack while lying in a hospital bed? She could not accept the doctor's findings; in her mind she kept thinking that something was wrong, but what? Could the report be in error? Did the examiner miss something? She just could not accept the finding of natural causes.

She went to the kitchen quickly ate a sandwich and drank a diet cola then headed to the study and logged on to the computer. Google searches on how to induce a heart attack and how to cause a heart were not very helpful. After about three hours of searching she gave up and readied herself to get some sleep. Sleep did not come easy this night. Her mind kept asking the questions "How could Jack have a heart attack" and "Why didn't the medical examiner find a cause?"

*****

The next day she had playground duty at St. Matthews with Yolanda Jones the school science teacher. As they observed the children at play, Gabriella asked if it is true that Yo had spent a year in medical school.

"Yes, I completed one year of med school then got pregnant with the twins. Had to take an extended maternity leave due to complications and difficulty during the pregnancy so now two pregnancies later I'm Yo Jones mother of four rather than Yo Jones medical doctor; but I have no regrets. Why the question?"

"Yesterday I got the medical examiner's report and his finding that Jack died of a heart attack. Somehow, Yo, I can not accept this. Something in me keeps telling me that Jack did not die of natural causes or of complications from the accident. From your medical studies and science background can you think of anything that would mimic the symptoms of a heart attack?"

"Oh that's an easy question. From my pharmacology course at Purdue I can tell you that an injection of potassium chloride would do the trick and leave no residuals that can be detected in an autopsy other than elevated levels of potassium in the blood which of course could be due to natural causes. Now that you ask I remember one night a group of us were having some beers at the Boiler Pit coming up with ways to commit the perfect murder. No one could top an injection of potassium. The only trace we came up with would be a small puncture wound at the site of the injection. But then if the chemical were introduced through an existing I.V line there would be no wound. Besides chances are in a normal autopsy the examiner would not be looking for such a tiny puncture."

Gabriella replied "Yo, that's interesting. The only thing the medical examiner noted other that the heart attack was an elevated level of potassium."

Just then the bell rang ending the recess period and the two teachers headed back to their classrooms. When Gabriella got home she phoned Gary and told him about the autopsy report and what Yo had told her about potassium chloride. They agreed that they would take their hunch to Mike Huest.

*****

It was four o'clock on Friday. Huest was finishing the booking of the suspect in the 14th Street burglary when Gary and Gabriella arrived to meet with him.

"Mike this is Gabriella Victor, Jack's widow."

"Pleasure to meet you, my condolences to you. I heard that your husband was a good man."

"Thanks, yes he was a good husband too."

Gary asked if he and Gabriella could have some time to talk with Mike about Jack's death.

"Sure, let's go into the meeting room." Mike led them into a small meeting room with a well worn square table and eight metal chairs. Three of the walls were lined with gray file cabinets and the other wall had a sink small refrigerator and of course a pot of strong stale coffee. After offering Gary and Gabriella some coffee they sat down around the old table. Mike began the conversation "OK, what do you have for me? The autopsy was pretty negative and indicated a natural cause of death."

"I can't accept the fact that my husband died of natural causes. He was in very good physical shape and health. The doctor gave me a good and optimistic report on his condition the afternoon Jack died. I can not accept the finding that my husband died from a heart attack. His last physical was four months before the accident. His doctor told Jack that he was in excellent health. His heart was strong; his cholesterol levels low nothing would indicate a future heart attack. I know that the medical examiner did find an elevated level of potassium in the blood and I have since learned that potassium chloride would cause heart failure and not leave any traces."

The detective's eyes lit up and one could tell from his expression that Gabriella's conviction in her voice had touched him and aroused his curiosity. He asks with the criminal investigator's tone; "So you think someone injected your husband with potassium; but who and why?"

Gabriella looked deeply into Gary's eyes and in a stern manner her body language told Gary not to mention the money from Rook and Rose.

"Mike we don't know." Gary had a difficult time lying to his friend but his devotion for Gabriella overrode his morals.

"Gary, that gives me a big problem. I have no suspect, no motive, and a coroner's report that says cause of death due to a heart attack. I got nothing to go on."

"Mike, it's just a hunch. But maybe someone, I don't know who, didn't like Jack's vote and leadership on the sale of the hospital or maybe an angry student. It's possible that someone became angry enough to kill him. Maybe that's a starting point. I know it's very weak, but both Gabriella and I somehow feel in our hearts that there was foul play involved in Jack's death."

The law enforcement training in the police lieutenant took over and he responded; "That's all well and good; but I need more than your hunch to build a case. I need evidence; give me some and I can start an investigation. Without a motive or cause of death my hands are tied. Given our department's case load if I began an investigation based on a hunch my superior will have my ass. Sorry Mrs. Victor but there is not much more I can do."

"Thank you for your time, lieutenant."

"Here's my card and cell phone number please call me if you come up with anything at all. And once again my sincere condolences."

*****

As the two drove back to the lake house Gary was trying to convince Gabriella that she must tell Mike about the bribe. "Gabby, you've got to tell Mike the whole story. That is the key to his opening an investigation. Without that information his hands are tied."

Gabriella was insistent that neither she nor Gary could ever tell the police about the money or the meeting with Rook.

"Gary, Jack has an excellent reputation as an honest and decent man. I will not do anything to tarnish his good name even if it means that my silence will let his killer get away with murder. I just can't do it!

116

Please do not mention this to anyone else. I told you in strict confidence because you and he were close friends. I beg you to respect his reputation."

"O.K. You want to stop at the Jib Room for some catfish and listen to the bluegrass?"

"Alright"

*****

The two had a catfish dinner and a few beers at the Jib Room, listened to some bluegrass and then headed home. Once again on the drive back to her house Gary's blood ran hot with passion. He so much wanted to take her in his arms and let her know his feelings for her. But once more, his friendship for Jack and the fear of offending Gabriella controlled his passion.

The weekend, as the past weekends went slowly for Gabriella. She finally could empty Jack's closet and sort out the things she would take to the Goodwill center on Monday. The task took much longer than necessary due to stopping every so often for a good cry and answering phone calls.

*****

Saturday morning found Lt. Huest at police headquarters finishing the paperwork on the arrest of Daniel Brewster on burglary charges not only in the 14th Street apartments but also the Varsity and Sta-

117

dium View apartments. Seems that Brewster was in the business of fencing personal computers and student based housing apparently was a good supply center. Getting a conviction on Brewster will be a cake walk compared to trying to find out if, who, how, and why someone murdered Jack Victor. Even though he had nothing to go on he kept thinking about the conviction in Gary's voice and the look in Gabriella's eyes. He knew that Gary was not a frivolous person and if he came to the police with something then in his heart he must have felt strongly about the matter. He was sure that Gary knew more than he was telling, but what? He began to jot down some theories on the board "Disgruntled student, upset board member or community citizen over sale, extreme case of road rage." All of these with big question marks behind them.

The thoughts were interrupted when Detective Don Mason stopped by Mike's desk. "Hey Mike, nice job on the Brewster case."

"Thanks, Don."

"Looks like you're already starting on the next case. Whatda you got?"

"Not much. I was just thinking about that Professor Victor who died in the hospital after a bad crash. I guess my detective instincts are asking how a healthy relatively young man on the road to recovery can suffer a massive heart attack. Right now just a curiosity."

"Have to agree it does sound strange. But hey, strange things happen. If I were you I'd work on an easier case. Lord knows we have plenty of crime. Seems to me the students are a wilder bunch this year. Maybe it's the football team's success. Use to be the students would celebrate the winning of the coin toss because it was the only thing the Cougars won on the football field. Well I'm outa here, see you on Monday."

"Yea, bye have a good weekend Don."

Mike went back to his desk and began to scribble some more notes.

*****

Monday morning Gabriella was getting ready to head off to class. She poured her glass of juice, cup of coffee and bowl of granola. She opened the *Herald* and there it was right beneath the fold- POLICE OPEN INVESTIGATION INTO PROFESSOR'S DEATH. The short article that followed merely said that the police were looking into Jack's death but they really had no hard evidence yet to suspect foul play or any persons of interest.

Gabriella's blood began to boil with anger- "Shit! Gary promised me he would keep this quiet. How could he violate our friendship? I never thought he would do such a thing merely for a story."

Just then the phone rang.

"Gabby, I know what you are thinking but I did not put that article in the *Herald*. Seems an overzealous intern either saw something when he was covering a story at the police department or talked to someone, but he came back to the newsroom and convinced the editor to plant the piece. Believe me I had nothing to do with this."

"Gary, I believe you. But this is just what I did not want to happen. If the police start looking into this they may discover the money and Jack's reputation will be ruined. I got to go to school now. Good-bye"

She hung up the phone. At this time neither she nor Gary knew that the short article would turn out to be fortuitous.

*****

Later that afternoon a scraggly unshaven man wearing a baseball cap with the inscription "Anglers do it on a hook" walked into the Midland Police station.

"Good afternoon sir can we help you?"

"Yep, I read in the *Herald* you guys think that prof. did not die from no accident. I reckon I should talk to the man in charge."

The desk sergeant picks up the telephone and dials the homicide division. Detective Mason answers the call as the desk sergeant asks if the police are investigating the Victor death. Mason tells the sergeant that there is no investigation but that Huest has an interest. "I'll see if Mike can talk to the guy."

A few moments later Mike Huest came into the lobby.

"This man says he needs to speak to the detective in charge of the Victor case."

"Hi I'm Lt. Huest. We really have no case yet but if you think you have some valuable information I will be happy to listen. You want to speak with me about the Victor death?"

"Yep. Can we go someplace private?"

"Sure come this way."

Huest leads the man through the security door and into one of the interrogation rooms; a 10 by 10 room with block walls, a one way mirror and a small window in the steel door. The light bulb dangling from the ceiling casts rotating shadows on the wall.

"Have a seat. What can you tell me?"

"Well, I don't know if it's important or not but I seen that E.R. doc Rook talking to a fella that looks like from the newspaper pictures to me that professor that got kilt. I aint hear what they was a talking about but from the way the doc was screamin and waving his hands it wern't friendly. I went over to talk with 'em and he shut up mighty quick. I got into my Jon boat and went behind a cove to catch some Crappie. could see them but they can't see me, I seen the doc grab that other guy by the shirt and waving his finger in the guy's face. I heard him say 'I'll see you dead first.' That's when I got outa there quick like. I didn't know what was gonna happen."

"How do you know it was Dr. Rook?"

"Cause I recognized him. He's the one that fixed my busted leg. It was Rook alright."

"Other than the apparent raucous what makes you remember the incident?"

"Oh I remember it ok. That doc got into his fancy sport car and sped off peeling rubber down the ramp way. Made such a noise I thought to my self 'Damn he's gonna scare all the fish with such a noise.' No, I remember it real well."

"Thanks for the information. You've been very helpful, now if I can get your name and a phone number where I can contact you if I need more information."

"Sure enough. Name's Jessie Farmer phone number 555 7169"

"Thanks again, I'll be in touch if we need anything.

If you think of anything else here's my card and cell phone number."

"Just tryin to do my duty."

Huest led the man back out into the corridor. They shook hands and the angler left. Well it wasn't much but the fisherman gave Huest his first lead. The next day he went to Rook's office to interview the staff. Nobody could provide much information until he talked with Sarah.

"Yes I remember when Dr. Rook had a meeting with Mr. Victor, it was on the14[th]."

"How can you be sure of the date?"

"Because I was working after hours using the office computer to write my policy analysis paper for my V160 Introduction to Public Affairs course. The paper was due on the 15th. Never did learn to start my papers before the last minute. Pulled an all nighter. Dr. Rook came in and did not say much. Usually he has a joke for us, but not that night. He just rushed past my desk and into his office. I noticed the light on phone line two lit up just after he got into the office. Don't know who he was talking to but from his body language he was not happy. Is Dr. Rook in some kind of trouble?"

"Just asking some routine questions. Thank you for your help."

The next day Huest visited Midland General to interview some of the staff in the E.R. His first stop was the Human Resources Department to find out who was working the E.R. the night Jack died. At first the receptionist was very reluctant to give him any information even though he identified himself as a police officer. She finally agreed to have him speak with the H.R. Director Jack Lee. Lee was cooperative and searched his database to find out who was working the E.R. that particular night and prints out a copy for the detective. As Mike scanned the list he noticed that Dr. Rook's name was not on the list. Mike then asks Lee which of the people on the list are working in the hospital today. Lee again checks his database and tells the detective that Barb Jennings an E.R. nurse was working the night in question and is on duty now.

"Where can I find Ms. Jennings?"

"Let's see she should be in the E.R. right now."

"Thank you for your help."

Huest went to the E.R to talk with Ms. Jennings. The shift coordinator told him she was on her lunch break and most likely sitting in the cafeteria. When he got to the cafeteria there were fortunately only a few nurses eating. He went to the closest table and asked if anyone knew Barb Jennings.

"Sure she's sitting over there next to the mural."

He approached the table flashed his badge and said "Ms. Jennings I'm Lt. Huest with the Midland Police mind if I sit down and ask you a few questions? I'll try not to disturb your dinner."

"No, please have a seat. What's this about?"

"Just a routine investigation at this time. Nothing special. What can you tell me about the night Professor Victor died?"

"Not too much I think he was on the general med-surg floor, I'm an E.R. nurse."

"Yes ma'am. Do you remember who the E.R doctor on duty was that night?"

"Yes, I thought it strange that both Dr. Ownes and Dr. Rook were working. Especially Dr. Rook. I remember telling one of the other nurses that this is the first time I saw Dr. Rook in the E.R during a Cougars home game. He's not only a big fan and season ticket holder but he's got some really good seats. Almost midcourt and at floor level. I recall that he left the E.R early that night. I thought he was heading for the game."

The other nurse sitting at the table gave Huest some important information.

"Excuse me officer but I remember seeing Dr. Rook

on 4 East. I was coming up from records and when the elevator stopped and the door opened on 4 East I saw Dr. Rook coming out of 415, Mr. Victor's room. I held the elevator door open waiting for him to come my way; but instead he just turned the other way and went down the back stairs. I thought maybe he was on an exercise kick or something. He normally stops to chat with nurses but not that night. Seemed to me he didn't want anyone to see him. He was in a hurry to get off the floor."

"Thank you ladies. You both were very helpful. Here are my cards and cell phone number, if you think of anything else please call me."

*****

Huest went back to the office to digest the information he received. He took out a yellow legal note pad from his desk and wrote down what he knew so far. First Rook and Victor had some form of altercation at the lake. The fisherman heard Rook threaten Victor. When Rook returned to his office he was visibly upset. Why did Rook work the E.R the night Victor died when he hadn't worked the E.R in a very long time? Was it merely coincidental that the man he threatens to kill, dies in his hospital on the only night Rook worked there? He was seen leaving room 415 shortly before Victor had the heart attack. Rook also has access to the hospital drugs and could have easily taken a vile or two of potassium chloride and he certainly knew how to administer the drug. From a former case he learned that Potassium chloride can induce a fatal heart attack and would leave no traces. He assumed Midland General would have a supply of the drug on hand and as an emergency physician on staff Rook would have access to the drug. He had opportunity, means but what was his motive? At the bottom of the page he wrote in big letters and circled the word "WHY???"

He was sure that Gary knew the answer to that question. He called Riggs.

"Gary, I put together some strong circumstantial evidence but there is one major piece missing from the puzzle- what was the killer's motive? Do you know any reasons why someone would want to kill Victor?"

There was a stark silence on the other end of the phone. Gary could not answer.

"Gary, come clean I need to know what you know? Come on Gary talk to me. I've got a feeling you know more than you're telling. I need to know everything you know to proceed with an investigation. I can't go only on hunches; the chief will be on my ass in no time. Gary you've got to tell me."

"Not over the phone Mike. Meet me at ten o'clock on the top floor of the city-county parking garage."

*****

Shortly before ten Gary backed his car into a parking stall on the northwest corner of the garage and nervously awaited the police officer. He remembered his promise to Gabriella that he would keep quiet; yet he also knew that without motive Huest did not have a very strong case. What to do? Does he violate his promise to Gabriella and risk any chance he might have to become her lover; or does he tell the story and help put Rook in jail? Before he could answer his own rhetorical question he sees headlights coming up the ramp onto the top floor. The black four door Ford pulls along side him and the passenger window rolls down. "OK Gary let's talk."

Gary gets into the front seat of the police vehicle. Stumbling for words he asks the detective to keep what he is about to tell him quiet until absolutely necessary.

"I'll do what I can because of what you did for us in that IAB incident but what you tell me will have to come out in the trial."

Of course Gary knew this. So reluctantly and very quietly he tells the detective all about the money and the vote.

*****

Huest returned to the police headquarters. He puts together what he has learned. The next morning he presented the case to his chief Leon Phillips. Phillips was skeptical. It was his typical modus operandi to play the role of devil advocate. He reminded Mike about the bad publicity and the heat from city hall if none of this were true. While Huest could not convince Phillips that he had enough to get a conviction he did convince the chief that he could bring Rook in for questioning and maybe break him. While Phillips did not totally buy into the plan, nonetheless he gave Mike the go ahead. Phillips tells the detective. "Hopefully Rook will slip up and render a confession. I'm counting on you to be good interrogator. Don't go easy on him. Good luck."

*****

The next day Huest and two uniformed officers went to the offices of Premier Health Group. They found Dr. Rook in his office at his desk talking with one of the other E. R. doctors.

As the police enter the office Rook shouts, "Hey what the hell do you think you're doing? You can't just come into my office."

"Yes sir we can. We would like you to come to headquarters to answer some questions about the Victor death. You can either come with us voluntarily or handcuffed and under arrest. What'll it be doc?"

Huest was hoping the doctor would come voluntarily. He did not think he had enough to make an arrest hold up. Fortunately the doctor took the bluff.

"Ok I'll go with you. Just don't let my staff see me go out of here in handcuffs, ok?"

"Sure doc."

The two uniformed officers put Rook in the back seat of a squad car and drove to the station. Huest followed in his unmarked vehicle. When they got to the station Huest escorted Dr. Rook into the same interrogation room where the fisherman gave him the opening lead.

"Please sit down Dr. Rook. Did you know a Jack Victor?"

"Yes he was chair of the hospital board. He and I worked together on plans for the expansion of the emergency department. Why?"

"I'll ask the questions. Now on the night Mr. Victor died were you working in the E.R.?"

"I don't recall the night, I may have why?"

"Did you and Mr. Victor have a meeting at the Lake that resulted in the two of you arguing?"

With that the physicians turned stark. He began to wrestle with his hands; his palms were beginning to become sweaty.

Huest sized on the opportunity. He knew he hit a raw nerve and was going to go in for the kill. In a loud and intimidating voice he asked, "Doc will you answer my question! You either had a meeting or you didn't! Yes or no which is it?"

Rook began to gain control over his emotions. After a long pause he told the detective, "Officer, the tone of your voice now leads me to believe that I may be a suspect in some crime. I want to go on record that I will not answer any more questions until my lawyer gets here"

"That certainly is your right. Here's the phone make your call."

While Dr. Rook was calling his lawyer, Mike took this opportunity to call Gary and tell him that he thinks he got a break in the case and brought Dr. Rook in for questioning. While he does not have a strong case he is sure Rook did it and that he could break Rook into a confession.

Gary then called Gabriella to tell her the good news.

"Gabby, I just got a call from Mike Huest. He brought Adam Rook in for questioning. He's feels pretty certain he's got the right man."

"Gary, I don't think so. I don't think Rook is Jack's killer. Can you come out here I want to show you something."

"Sure be right over."

*****

Back at police headquarters a neatly attired white haired man handed Huest his business card and held out his hand.

"My name is Thaddeus Wilson and I will be representing Dr. Rook. I would like a few minutes to confer with my client."

"Sure counselor he's right in here"

The lawyer sat down across the table from Rook and the two men talked quietly. Shortly the lawyer exited and confronted Huest.

"Detective either book Dr. Rook or release him."

"He's free to go for now. But inform your client not to leave the state."

*****

About a half hour after her telephone call, Gary got to Gabriella's.

"Gary I want to show you this. Tom Langdon from Jack's school brought me Jack's office computer. He wanted me to view Jack's files and make copies of anything I wanted to keep before they cleaned the disk to re-issue the computer. I found a folder that was password protected, the only folder on the disk that was protected. I recall Jack sharing with me that he often used part of my maiden name and our wedding date as a password for personal data. I tried "kis1123" and sure enough I got in. Look. There is a flow of letters to Naomi Hoag. Jack found out from a colleague friend of his at Barry University that Naomi never completed the MHA program but instead was asked to leave the program after the second semester. But she still listed the MHA degree on her C.V. The degree was one of the major prerequisites for the Midland position. Look at this note. It's dated just two days before the crash. Jack told Naomi that time was running out and unless she resigned her position as CEO for 'personal' reasons he was going to expose her fraud to the board and recommend her immediate termination due to cause. Somehow I think she is the one behind this but I can't tie all the ends together. If she killed Jack in the hospital it seems too much of a coincidence that he had an accident two weeks before the board meeting and ended up at Midland General."

"I agree, Gabby that does seem like a mighty odd coincidence. What do we know about the driver of the car that hit Jack, uh, a Billie Franklin?"

"Not much. All I know is that his injuries were not life threatening. I think he stayed in the hospital a few days. I recall the Sherriff's deputy telling me that the car was registered to a Billie Franklin in Orlando Florida. But that's all I knew. Really didn't want to know more about him."

"I know one of the reporters working for the *Orlando Sentinel*. Let me call him and see if he can find anything out about Bill Franklin."

Gary opened his cell phone and dialed 863 555 3908.

A computer message welcomed him to the newspaper "If you know your party's extension please dial it now. If not enter the last name by using the telephone dial pad or wait on the line and an operator will be with you shortly."

Gary punched in BASSET.

"Hello this is Tom Basset."

"Tom, Gary Riggs here I'm a reporter with the Midland *Herald*. We met at the regional conference last year."

"Oh yea you're the Makers Mark on rocks with a twist guy. Never forget what a man drinks. Why the call?"

"Tom, I need some information. I'm working on a story that involves a former resident of the Orlando area a Billie Franklin aged about 27. I was wondering if you could do a background check for me."

"Will do. Do I get part of the Pulitzer?"

"Not that big of a story. If you find out anything call

me at 812-555-3207. Thanks for your help on this; I'll buy you a Jack Daniels next time we meet."

"Deal, y'all take care and I'll be in touch."

Gary then dialed the office of the University Highway Research Safety Center.

"Good afternoon HRSC this is Norma how may I direct your call?"

"Eric Cornwell please."

"May I tell him who's calling?"

"This is Gary Riggs."

Shortly Eric Cornwell answered. Dr. Cornwell is the head of the Accident Reconstruction Division of the Highway Research Safety Center and a noted mechanical engineer who reconstructs motor vehicle crashes for the National Highway Traffic Safety Administration. The two first met when Gary was covering the NASCAR beat. Cornwell is a member of the NASCAR accident investigation team.

"Gary, long time no see."

"It's been awhile, glad you remember me."

"Hey read your column all the time. What can I do for you?"

"Do you remember the crash on Lake Road a few months ago that killed the college professor Jack Victor?"

"Yea, I remember reading about that. Bizarre crash, I couldn't figure out how a car driving at the slow speed as reported in the *Herald* could have suffered so much damage. Why do you ask?"

"Jack was personal friend. I share your apprehensions. Do you think you could review the crash report and let me know what you find?"

"Sure. I was planning on doing some work on Saturday; I'll just fit a quick look into my routine. I'll call you as soon as I find something out. What's a good number, I hate calling the paper always on hold for a long time?"

"Thanks Eric, call me on my cell 555-3207."

"Will do."

Gary left Gabriella and went to the office to finish up a story on invasive weed control on Lake Lincoln.

*****

The following Monday Gary got a call from Orlando.

"Gary, Tom here. Hope I didn't wake you up, I hear

you Yankees sleep half the day."

"Hey, been up at least two hours. Did you find anything?"

"Sure did, not sure it's gonna be any help though. Seems that Franklin kid was quite a character. I found out some interesting stuff from a contact at the University of Central Florida that he attended the college for two semesters. Now the following must be off the record. My contact broke university and federal law in telling me that Franklin got booted out for repeatedly violating the student code of ethics regarding alcohol and drugs. Seemed he had quite a drinking problem. He got arrested four times on everything from DUI to possession and dealing. Strange thing is that he was tried by Judge Bridges who around this part is known as a hard ass. That man usually throws the book at druggies but this time he put Franklin on probation and under the guardianship of a Ms. Naomi Hoag. I found that to be interesting so I did a background check on her. Seems she's a divorcee and her maiden name was Franklin. She's the boy's aunt. About three months later our paper reported that she and the judge were having an affair. She left town shortly after that. Didn't find out where she went, but I can do some more checking if you like."

"No Tom, that won't be necessary, we know where she is. Thank you very much, this was extremely helpful."

"No problem next time we meet you owe me a double. You gonna be in Atlanta next month?"

"Can't make Atlanta, sorry but I still owe you the double. Thanks again see you."

"Sorry 'bout Atlanta, y'all write a great story you hear. Send me a copy, bye."

Gary put down the phone and pondered the link between Hoag and Franklin. He was now more convinced than ever that the crash was not accidental. Hopefully Eric Cornwell will be able to confirm his suspicion.

He went back to writing how the spread of the weeds could eventually strangle the lake. However, he was not very productive. His mind kept wandering off to the Hoag-Franklin connection.

Later that afternoon Eric Cornwell called him with the information he wanted.

"Mr. Riggs, Eric Cornwell."

"Yes, Dr. Cornwell do you have anything?"

"I think I do. I reviewed the data collected by the sheriff's office, the accident report and the photos taken of both vehicles at the scene. The estimated speed of vehicle one, the professor's car, in my opinion was not fast enough to provide sufficient momentum to go over the bream in the road shoulder and continue to travel down the ravine and roll-over as it did. Also the indentations and scratch patterns on both vehicles correlated very highly with the indentations and scratch patterns on the experimental cars we tested for NASCAR. Such a correlation would be due to chance less than 5% of the time which is the standard acceptance for a significant finding. If I were looking at these data for NASCAR I would conclude that the driver of vehicle two deliberately struck the left front quarter panel of vehicle one with such force and intent as to force vehicle one into the wall or in this case down the ravine."

"Thank you Dr. Cornwell, would it be possible to get a written copy of your findings?

"Norma is typing one up as we speak. I thought you would need one. This is an interesting case and the first time I was able to apply my data and crash model to a non-race situation. I might just turn this into a publication."

Hanging up the phone Gary reviewed what he learned so far. Naomi Hoag and Billy Franklin were relatives. Franklin had a past arrest record and the crash that resulted in Jack's death was not accidental. Gary thought about this all night and the next morning shared his new found information with Gabriella. She arranged to meet him in town and together they would visit Huest.

*****

After having a cup of coffee at the Loaf and Cup they walked across the street to police headquarters to give the information to Huest.

Mike Huest was not happy to hear their new theory. "Look I went out on limb for you two with the Rook lead, got my ass busted on that one. You better have something solid this time else I'll be back writing parking tickets." Huest was not too excited to see them and reluctant to go further with an investigation.

After some persuasion the detective agreed to see what he could do. He told them that this time he was not going to do anything without his boss's ok. He prepared his pitch to Phillips in his head a couple of times and then walked into the chief's office. After about an hour he finally convinced Phillips that they had enough evidence with Cornwell's statement to bring Franklin in on at least a vehicular charge.

Along with two uniformed police officers Huest went to the 16th street address and brought Franklin in for questioning. They put him in the same small interrogation room where the fisherman earlier had told of the encounter at the lake with Rook and Victor.

"Sit down, you want some coffee?"

Franklin had been in the system long enough to know to avoid drinking any liquids. He knew they would keep him alone in the room hoping the kidneys would weaken his will to remain silent.

"No I want a lawyer. I ain't saying nothing until my mouthpiece gets here!"

Huest leaves and came back with a telephone and phone book. He plugged the phone into a jack and said, "Here call what ever lawyer you like."

"I ain't got no lawyer and no money to pay one. I want one of them pubic defenders."

Huest left while Franklin sat in the stark room. He sat motionless knowing that the cops were watching his every move through the one way mirror on the wall and would be interpreting his body language. His experiences with the police told him not to show signs of fear as these would be interpreted as expressions of guilt. He knew they would make him wait as long as possible.

About an hour later a man entered the interrogation room and introduced himself to Franklin.

"Mr. Franklin I'm Michael Thompson from the public defenders office. Officers may I have a few moments alone to confer with my client?"

"Sure."

The two men conferred for about 20 minutes and then the lawyer opened the door and Huest and prosecutor Carol Berry entered the room. Berry began the dialog.

"Mr. Franklin, here's the story. We know you deliberately ran Professor Victor's car off the road with such violence and malice as to cause injuries so severe as to result in his ultimate death. In other words you killed him! We are going to charge you with vehicular homicide. I will be asking the court for a maximum prison term. At best you're looking at a long time in Michigan City and perhaps a needle injection at Terre Haute; of course I have no idea what the state of Florida will do with you. In a nutshell, Mr. Franklin you are in big trouble."

"What are you offering my client, Ms. Berry?"

"Let's see what he tells us. If we like it, and it's good I grant immunity and not report this to Florida. This is a one time offer Mr. Thompson. Advise your client to take the deal or we will see each other in court."

Thompson leaned over and whispered something into Franklin's ear. After a short dialog between the lawyer and his client Franklin told Berry all that he knew and what happened on Lake Road.

"Look this wasn't my idea. I had no beef with that prof guy. Didn't even know him. It was my aunt Naomi that put me up to it. She told me to bang into him and run his car into a tree. She wanted him dead. If I didn't do it she would go back to the judge in Florida and tell him that I was using and dealing again. I'm looking at 20 years. I was scared I knew she was sleeping with the judge and he'd do it too. I had no choice. It was her fault she made me do it. I ain't gonna take a needle for that mean bitch!"

Carol Berry said "I'll have the papers prepared."

Shortly the court recorder entered with the transcript of Franklin's statement. Thompson reviewed the document and advised his client to sign it.

"Lt. Huest, pick up Naomi Hoag for the murder of Jack Victor."

Once again Huest and two uniformed officers went to the hospital to make an arrest. After showing their identification the three men entered the office of the Hospital CEO.

"Ms. Naomi Hoag you're under the arrest for the death of Jack Victor. Anything you say can and will be used against you in a court of law. You have the right to an attorney, if you can not afford one, one will be appointed by the court. Place your hands behind your back please."

With that one of the uniformed officers placed her in handcuffs and led her out to the corridor. On the way out Naomi Hoag looked at her long time secretary Bonnie.

"Call my lawyer Sam Goldenbaum, tell him to come to police headquarters."

*****

Shortly after she was booked, Mr. Samuel Goldenbaum arrived at police headquarters. Goldenbaum was a senior partner in the firm of Marr Quatman and Silvers which is the largest law firm in the state. It gained notoriety when the firm won a not guilty verdict for a local professional basketball player accused of stabbing his live in girl friend fifteen times resulting in her ultimate death. Even with the accused's fingerprints on the weapon and a strong motive Goldenbaum was able to win the case by arguing that a teammate also had motive and thus created sufficient reasonable doubt in the jurors' minds to render a not guilty verdict. After talking with Hoag he felt that this case was a piece of cake.

*****

The next day the headlines of the *Herald* read **HOSPITAL CEO ARRESTED IN DEATH OF PROFESSOR.** The story that followed merely talked about how the police arrested Hoag but gave little information on the evidence to be presented in the trial. Berry was playing these cards close to her vest.

Once again unwittingly a story on page one proved beneficial to Huest's case. About mid-morning Lt.

Huest had a visitor.

"Good morning I'm Lt. Huest, how can I help you"

"My name is Donna Cobble and I'm a nurse on 4 east at the hospital."

"Four east, isn't that the wing with room 415?"

"Yes. The night that Mr. Victor died I was working the evening shift. I went into Mr. Victor's room to check his vitals and I saw Ms Hoag by the sharps container. When she saw me she turned pale and then yelled at me for not emptying the container as scheduled. I thought this a bit odd since the container was replaced that morning as scheduled. She angrily left in a huff. I did not think any more about it until I read the morning paper. Do you think she did it and put the syringe in the container?"

"I really cannot comment on an ongoing case. But thank you very much for coming forward. If we need anymore information we will contact you."

"You're welcome. I just want to see justice served."

A few days later in Superior Court the attorney and his client stood before Judge Barnes at an arraignment hearing.

"Ms. Hoag you have been charged with the murder of Mr. Jack Victor. In this matter how to you plead?"

"Not guilty"

"Your honor, my client is a respected member of the community and CEO of the only hospital in town. I petition that she be released on her own recognizance."

"Your honor the state vehemently objects. Ms. Hoag is charged with a capital offense and poses a grave flight risk. Furthermore…"

"At ease Ms. Berry. Motion denied. Ms. Berry is correct this is a capital case and she is to be held in the county jail pending the commencement of her trial. Trial date set for two months from today. That's all."

Chapter 7
The Trial

Carol Berry spent the weekend preceding the trial date reviewing her courtroom strategy. She still was not convinced whether or not she should call Dr. Lambini to testify. Dr. Lambini is the pathologist who performed the autopsy. He would have to testify that he did not find any toxic substances other than an elevated level of potassium.

She knew that Goldenbaum would surely play this up and make a production number of it and if Carol does not call Lambini to the stand than Goldenbaum would most certainly. On the other hand, if he were a defense witness then she could easily introduce the issue of potassium chloride and its effects. She would be able to control the flow of this important bit of information.

One year to the day of that fatal crash on Lake Road the bailiff of the Lincoln County superior court asked that all present rise.

"In the matter of the State vs. Naomi Hoag this court is now in session the Honorable Mary Margret Hill presiding."

Judge Hill had a reputation as a fair but no nonsense judge. Both attorneys were very familiar with the way in which she ran a trial and knew that everything they did must be done strictly by the book.

"In the matter of the state versus Naomi Hoag are both attorneys prepared to proceed?"

Both Carol Berry and Samuel Goldenbaum responded in the affirmative. That first day the judge heard a series of motions from Goldenbaum to dismiss some of the evidence the state used in making the case against Naomi Hoag. In each instance the judge dismissed the objections. Her final ruling was that the court would adjourn for the day and jury selection set to begin the next day.

Jury selection took the full day. Surprisingly jury selection went quickly for a murder trial. Goldenbaum used both of his preemptory challenges while Berry used one of hers. One jury candidate was dismissed because she took a class with Jack Victor. Another candidate was dismissed because she was eight and a half months pregnant.

"We will be hearing opening arguments when court resumes tomorrow at 9:00 a.m. This session is now adjourned."

Gabriella and Gary met with Carol Berry outside the courtroom.

"I think things went well today. While you never get your perfect jury, I'm satisfied with the jurors we have. I like the seven male and five females. From my observance of their behavior today I think they will be paying attention and heavily weigh the facts. Well you both get a good night's sleep we have an important day ahead of us."

"Thank you Carol, see you tomorrow."

*****

Carol Berry went back to her apartment to rewrite her opening arguments for the fifth time. She still did not feel comfortable about the Lambini tactic. Even though she was an experienced and successful prosecutor, she still got the opening day jitters the eve of a big trial. The one thing that would get her through is remembering the words of Laurence Olivier when asked if he still got nervous before performing Shakespeare replied- "If I do not get nervous I know I will not perform well."

Needless to say Carol Berry did not get much rest that evening. Neither did Gabriella. She was awake all night recalling the events of one year ago and the frightful ringing of the telephone and the long trip to Midland General. The pain still gnawed at her. Maybe she thought when the trial is ended and the nightmare over she can then have some peace. Maybe then she can get her life back to some sense of normalcy. She knew that Jack would have wanted her to get on with her life and find a new meaningful relationship. He always said she should do whatever made her happy.

*****

Judge Hill opened the trial promptly at 9:00 a.m. Carol Berry rose from her desk and walked slowly toward the jury box. She looked into the eyes of each of the twelve members and in a quiet but yet firm voice began to outline the state's case. She told them that they would hear from experts that Jack Victor's heart attack was induced. They would learn that the crash was not accidental and that only Naomi Hoag had motive, opportunity and means. By now her voice rising to a crescendo: "We will present you with the evidence leading to no other decision than guilty as charged!"

Goldenbaum took another approach. He was dressed in a double breasted dark blue muted stripe suit, and yellow power tie. He spoke with an air of confidence almost cockiness that might be better suited to a New York city held trial rather than one in this small Midwest college town. He began by showing how the evidence against his client was merely circumstantial and none of it conclusive. He kept stressing the fact that the jury must find his client guilty beyond any reasonable doubt and that the burden of proof rested with the state and not with his client.

"My dear ladies and gentlemen of the jury. The prosecutor in this trial told you about the evidence she is going to be presenting, but I will remind you, just as the judge will that you must find my client guilty beyond a reasonable doubt. Yes beyond a reasonable doubt that she is guilty as charged. Not likely to have committed the crime for which she is charged, but guilty beyond any possible doubt. If there is any doubt that someone else might have done this horrendous act then you must acquit. Yes, no matter what your personal beliefs are, if you think that the facts do not fit you must find my client not guilty. This is your duty and our American right."

"The state will call its first witness" with these words the trial of Naomi Hoag began.

Carol began her argument- "The state calls Dr. Brad King." Dr King took his seat and was sworn in as Carol began her questioning.

"Dr. King, were you Professor Victor's primary care physician?"

"Yes I treated him for about five years."

"And how would you describe his state of health?"

"I would say that he was in excellent health. One of the few patients who regularly exercised and watched his diet. Yes he was very fit."

"Dr. King what was the condition of Professor Victor's heart?"

"Excellent"

"When was the last time you examined him, gave him a full physical?"

"About three months before the crash. His blood results were all negative, prostate fine. I even took an EKG to establish a baseline for future reference. Everything was normal. I found no problems. I told him to keep up the good work."

"No further question, your honor."

"Does defense wish to cross?"

"Yes. Now Dr. King, you stated that Mr. Victor was in good health when he left your office. Now in your years of experience have you ever had a patient seemingly in good health when he left your office die three months later?"

"I'm not sure"

"Come come Dr. King surely in your years of practice this has happened a few times."

"I suppose so but…"

"Thank you doctor no further questions"

Goldenbaum already planted the first seed of doubt.

"The state will call its next witness"

Carol sat at her desk still debating whether to call Dr. Lambini or not.

"Miss Berry, do you intend to call another witness or not?"

"Yes, your honor. The state wishes to call…." After a long pause and hesitation finished the sentence,

"The state calls Dr. Marcus Lambini to the stand."

After Dr. Lambini was sworn Berry began her questioning.

"Dr. Lambini you performed an autopsy on the body of Mr. Victor and determined the cause of death to be a myocardial infarction is this correct?'

"Yes"

"Now you heard Dr. King testify that Mr. Victor was in excellent physical condition. How could someone at his age and in good medical condition suffer such a massive heart attack?"

"The heart is a complicated organ. The stress of the crash, or surgery or a myriad of other reasons could trigger a malfunction."

"Can a heart attack be induced?"

"Yes, there are a number of chemicals and medications that can induce a heart attack, one such compound is potassium chloride."

"So, potassium chloride could cause the heart to fail. Did you find evidence of potassium in Professor Victor's blood?"

"Yes. I found a slight elevation but the blood of a healthy individual would show signs of blood potassium."

"So doctor, an injection of potassium chloride could have caused Professor Victor's heart to fail and give all impression of a heart attack?"

"Yes, that is correct."

"Thank you doctor. No further questions."

Goldenbaum had few questions to ask Dr. Lambini. He acknowledged the fact that Lambini is a qualified and highly respected pathologist

"Dr. Lambini how would the potassium have gotten into the victim's blood?"

"Most likely by injection."

"Most likely by injection, and who injected the victim, say a nurse on duty?"

"Objection leading"

"Objection sustained"

"Let me repeat the question- Do you know who injected the drug?"

"No"

"Could it have been one of the nurses?"

"Possibly"

"One of the doctors?"

"Again yes it is possible."

"Thank you doctor. No further questions."

"The state calls Eric Cornwell to the stand."

"Would you please state your name and occupation for the court?"

"Yes my name is Eric Cornwell and I am a research scientist with the university's Highway Research Safety Center and also the director of the Center's accident reconstruction division."

"Dr. Cornwell about how many publications do you have that describe how to reconstruct crashes and the interpretation of data?"

Goldenbaum rises

"Your honor the defense will concede Mr. Cornwell's credentials as an accident reconstructionist"

"Dr Cornwell. Did you analyze the data from a crash involving Jack Victor and Billie Franklin?"

"Yes, according to my analysis vehicle one…"

"Vehicle one that's the car driven by Professor Victor?"

"Yes, and we refer to the car driven by Mr. Franklin as vehicle two. According to my analysis vehicle one, that is Professor Victor's, was traveling at a very slow speed and braking at the time of impact. Vehicle one was traveling so slow that without a severe impact the car would not have sufficient momentum to cross the shoulder and rollover as it descended the ravine. I think the young saplings lining the roadway would have stopped the car."

"So in your expert opinion, doctor, Professor Victor's car was struck so hard as to force the car down the ravine."

"That is correct."

"Now you also analyzed the damage patterns of both vehicles and the scratch patterns did you not?"

"Yes. I analyzed the damage to vehicle one that is Professor Victor's car and vehicle two the one driven by Mr. Franklin and the resultant scratch patterns match fairly closely with the patterns derived in laboratory crashes. As you can see in these photographs there is a very good similarity in the pattern of the test vehicle and the standard. In fact the correlation was .64 and a value that large could have been a result of chance alone in less that 5% of the time. That is the accepted level of significance for scientific research. Our analysis is similar to that performed by a ballistics expert in determining whether or not a bullet was fired from the subject gun."

"Is it safe to conclude then that in your expert opinion the car driven by Mr. Franklin deliberately rammed Professor Victor's car?

"Yes I would conclude that."

"Thank you doctor. I have no further questions."

"Does the defense wish to cross?"

"Yes, your honor."

Goldenbaum approached the witness stand hands folded in front of him, glasses resting on the tip of his nose.

"Now Dr. Cornwell isn't it a law of science that cause and effect conclusions can not be made from correlations?"

"Yes, but in…."

"Thank you doctor. If the data were from- say a NASCAR race, could you interpret these data as indicating conclusively that the driver deliberately rammed into another car with the sole purpose of forcing the driver into the wall?"

"Well, no not conclusively but I…"

"So, you would not use your data to suspend a race car driver but have no qualms about using that data to send an innocent woman to jail!"

"Objection your honor!"

"Objection sustained. The jury will disregard defense counsel's remarks. Mr. Goldenbaum henceforth please save your editorial comments for summation. Any further questions for this witness?"

"No your honor."

"The defense now calls Mr. Billie Franklin to the stand."

Franklin took the witness stand and swore to tell the truth.

"Mr. Franklin could you tell us whether or not on the night of the crash you followed Professor Victor from the university to Lake Road; and then what happened on Lake Road?"

"That night I waited in the parking lot until he came out of the building and got into his car. As he drove out of the parking lot I followed him."

"Describe what happened on Lake Road."

"As we turned onto the road I got closer and closer. He slowed down and I hit his bumper."

"You say you struck his car, was this deliberate?"

"Yea. I was hoping he would speed up and lose control as he went around the bend, but instead he just slowed down."

"Then what happened?"

"I pulled along side him, he gave me the finger and I quick turned the steering wheel to the right, our front fenders were riding together for awhile then we went off the shoulder and down the ditch. My car went down and hit a tree."

"Mr. Franklin, why did you do this?"

"My aunt made me do it. She said she would like to see him dead and I should make it look like an accident. She said if I didn't do it she would tell the judge in Florida that I was using again and violated my probation. I was looking at 10-20 in Florida."

"And who is your aunt, the one that told you to attempt to kill Mr. Victor?"

"Naomi Hoag."

"No further questions your honor."

"Mr. Franklin you at one time were a student at Central Florida University is that not correct?"

"Yes"

"Did you graduate?"

"No"

"Why not?"

"I was kicked out."

"And what were the reasons for your expulsion?"

"I snorted some coke and got drunk"

"So you used cocaine and abused alcohol. About how many times?

"A few"

"A few. According to university police records you

were arrested four times. Are the police records erroneous?"

Franklin hesitated then responded in a low voice-"No."

"Mr. Franklin did Ms Berry offer you some deal in exchange for your testimony?"

Franklin sat quietly looking at Carol Berry.

"Your honor, please ask the witness to answer my question."

"The witness will answer the question."

"Yea. She said she'd charge me with vehicular homicide. But if I told her what I knew she would give me immunity and not report it to Florida. But I ain't lying, my aunt told me to kill that college dude!"

"Thank you Mr. Franklin."

After Billie Franklin testified Judge Hill declared a recess for lunch.

"Court will reconvene at 1:30"

To avoid the reporters gathered outside the courthouse Berry, Gabriella and Gary had some sandwiches brought in. They began eating when Goldenbaum entered the room.

"Excuse me for interrupting your lunch but I would like to talk with you. Carol you know that you don't have enough evidence to get a conviction on first degree murder. You know I can create a lot of doubt in the jury. I only need one. Let's save the County some money and you and I a lot of time and reach some kind of middle ground. My client will be willing to plea to involuntary with 3-5."

Before Carol could give an answer, Gabriella shouted.

"Go to hell! That bitch killed my husband. She deserves the needle. Three to five years is nothing compared to the loss I suffered."

"Well Sam I guess you have your answer."

"Bon appetite. As the saying goes see you in court. Mrs. Victor I understand your sorrow and feelings but I am afraid when this is all over you will wish you had taken our offer."

Goldenbaum left the three with the arrogance and confidence he displayed throughout the trial.

"That bastard! Carol do everything you can to nail that bitch's tail to the wall."

"I'll do my best, but between you and me Sam is one hell of a lawyer. He can sway a jury and he's right all he needs is one weak link."

The three finished their lunches in silence. At 1:25 they left the small meeting room and headed down the corridor to court room one.

"Hear Ye Hear Ye Session 23-671 of Superior court is now in session, the honorable Judge Hill presiding, all rise."

"Ms. Berry call your next witness."

"I call Mrs. Gabriella Victor to the stand."

"Mrs. Victor, when the university brought over Professor Victor's computer what did you do?"

"I opened most of the files and made copies of his papers, class notes and anything I wanted to keep or thought important."

"And in doing so did you not find a password protected file."

"Yes. I remember Jack telling me that he sometimes used a special password and when I entered the one he shared with me I was granted access to the files."

"I would like you to look at this set of printouts and tell me if these were the protected files you read."

Gabriella looked them over and asserted that they are indeed the printouts she made from Jack's computer. Carol Berry asked her to describe for the jury the contents. She then told about the finding from

Barry University showing that Hoag did not have the graduate degree she claimed and the memo Jack sent to Naomi threatening to go to the Board with the information he found unless she resigned.

"The state presents these as State exhibits 9, 10 and 11."

"Mrs. Victor, what were Jack's days like leading up to the crash?"

"He was frightened of something. I recall that two days before the crash Naomi Hoag called and they talked for a long time. I could not hear what she said but Jack was very irritated. The conversation got heated. When he hung up he was very upset. He told me at the next board meeting he had to do something he regretted doing."

Goldenbaum did not cross examine. He wanted to but in his crafty way he knew that if he attacked the grieving widow he'd lose sympathy with the jury. He was counting on his charm winning this case. He wasn't about to jeopardize that.

"We call Donna Perkins to the stand. Ms. Perkins please tell the court where you work."

"I' m a night shift nurse at Midland General assigned to 4 east."

"Four east, is that the wing where Mr. Victor was?"

"Yes room 415."

"On the night in question please tell us what you saw."

"I was assigned rooms 413 to 427. I went into 415 to take Mr. Victor's vitals and check his I.V. I saw Ms. Hoag by the sharps container. When she saw me she got quite embarrassed and agitated. She started yelling at me saying something about the container not being replaced in accordance with JCAHO standards. And then she left in a huff. I was put out by her behavior so I checked the sharps container and it had been replaced that morning. I could only see three used syringes in the container. When I checked Mr. Victor's chart I noticed that he was only given two injections that day. I thought someone had made a charting error. I checked the medical cabinet and drawer assigned to room 415 and the inventory was only two less than the previous count."

"So then there was one more syringe in the sharps container than injections recorded as being given to Mr. Victor."

"Yes"

"But how could that be?"

"Well I would say someone gave him something he was not intended to have."

"Objection- calls for speculation on the part of the witness."

"Sustained the jurors will disregard the final answer."

"Now Ms. Perkins do you know what medications or drugs were in those syringes?"

"Yes. I was suspicious and afraid I would be accused of malpractice so I sent the syringes to the lab for testing. One needle showed deposits of potassium chloride"

"Are you positive it was potassium?"

"Yes I made a copy of the lab report and gave it to the police lieutenant."

"Your honor the state wishes to enter the laboratory report as exhibit twelve."

"I have no further questions"

"Mr. Goldenbaum do you care to cross?"

"Yes your honor. Thank you. Now how many nights was Mr. Victor a patient of yours?"

"He came down from ICU and was in 415 for three nights."

"So he was there for three nights?"

"Yes"

"Miss Perkins how many hours had you worked the night before Mr. Victor suffered a heart attack?"

"Twelve"

"And how long was your shift the night he died?"

"Twelve"

"So you worked two twelve hour shifts in a thirty six hour period, weren't you a bit tired on that second night?"

"Uh, not too tired, I regularly work twelve hour shifts."

"Ms. Perkins you have more than one patient, I would guess you have many and being an evening duty nurse you most likely see many visitors coming and going is that not correct?"

"Yes"

"So then Ms. Perkins how can you be certain that the night you say you saw my client in 415 was the night of his death and not the night before, after all you were pretty tired?"

"I remember that day and all that happened very well. The next day my husband's guard unit left for combat duty. Two weeks later he was killed. I recall everything that happened the last day I saw my husband alive."

Goldenbaum had not expected this. He had hoped he could cause some confusion and thus create more doubt in the jurors' minds. He violated a cardinal rule of the defense bar- never ask a question if you are not sure of the answer. His question created, in the jurors' minds, sympathy for a grieving widow. If he attacked her further he would be perceived as hard hearted and lose the credibility he was trying to establish with the jury. He had no other choice

Carol Berry then said, "No further questions. The prosecution rests."

Judge Hill recessed court for the night.

"The defense will begin its arguments tomorrow at 9:00 a.m... This court is recessed."

*****

Carol Berry went back to her office to work on her closing and tried to anticipate Goldenbaum's tactics. So far his strategy was to create doubt in the minds of the jurors. She knew that his most effective approach was to get at least one juror to have reasonable doubt. She knew she did not have the strongest of cases. Her evidence was mostly circumstantial. If she could cross examine Hoag she was confident she could break her on the stand. Around the hospital the CEO had a reputation as somewhat of a hot head with an uncontrollable temper. Berry was looking forward to cross examining her she was convinced she could get into the defendant's head and make her slip up and say something incriminating. If Carol could let the jury see that fury then she would have a better chance of convincing the jurors that Hoag was at least capable of murder.

Carol reread the defense list of witness for the third time but Goldenbaum's witness list did not contain Hoag's name. Apparently he was not going to call her to testify in her own behalf. Carol thought that if she were defending rather than prosecuting she would not allow Hoag to testify either.

*****

Gary and Gabriella had dinner at a small family run informal Italian style restaurant near the lake. Gabriella said she was not too hungry and ordered a large salad, Gary ordered the steak pizzaiola.

"Care for a carafe of a Pinot Grigio?"

"Not tonight, Gary, I'm not in the mood for wine. This trial thing has me bummed out. I am afraid that Goldenbaum is going to get her off. He's such a good lawyer, I like Carol but she's young and I'm not sure a good match for the crafty Goldenbaum. I keep looking at the jurors' eyes I think they have a lot of doubt and don't believe it was murder. I think all that technical jargon from Cornwell confused the hell out of them. If she gets away with what she did to Jack and me, I don't know how I will react. She hurt us so much. Maybe I should have told Carol to take the plea agreement, and then at least she would have gotten some jail time and a ruined reputation. That would have at least been minimal justice. Going scot free is not right. I don't know."

"Gabby, Carol is crafty. She'll come up with some good tactics. I think she's held her own against Goldenbaum."

The waiter then arrived with their meals. "Madam you had the salad? And the steak pizzaiola for the gentleman."

They both ate the meals in silence. When they finished Gary drove her to the lake house. On the drive home Gabriella was extremely quiet. She just stared out the front window with a glassy eyed glaze. Gary was glancing over at her and wondering to himself what a beautiful woman she was even in this stressful time. He so much wanted to stop the car and tell her how much he loved her and to even make out like a couple of star struck teenagers. But he knew better, this was not the right time. He also knew that as a young attractive widow it would not be long before she found another love and once again his love for her would not be rewarded. He did not know how he would be able to cope with losing her a second time.

They arrived home he opened her door and walked

her to the front entrance said good-bye and drove back to town. On the way home he kept thinking about how much he loved Gabriella but sensed that she was still deeply in love with Jack. He could not compete with Jack when he was alive and could not compete with his memory. No matter what, he would still be in love with her. Just being with her these past months gave him a joy he had not felt before. Oh he thought how wonderful it would be to spend all his moments with her and to feel her warm body next to his. He yearned to wake every morning and see her next to him. If only he were to be so lucky.

*****

At nine o'clock Judge Hill opened the trail again in her usual manner. It was now the defense's opportunity to argue. As his first witness Goldenbaum called Professor Patrick Roberts to the stand. Roberts was Eric Cornwell's counterpart at the Safety Research Institute in Ann Arbor. After asking him questions to establish Roberts' credibility, Goldenbaum then went on to lead the professor into a critique of Cornwell's research. It was then Carol Berry's turn to cross.

"Mr. Roberts, did not your research institute also bid for the NHTSA contract to be the quality control center for Region Five?"

"Yes."

"And on the contract proposal, who was listed as the principal investigator?"

"I was."

"And that was the contract that was awarded to Dr. Cornwell, correct?"

"Yes."

"What happened at the SRI after it failed to win the NHTSA contract?"

"We had to lay off some staff including some research scientists."

"Mr. Roberts I would like you to look at this copy of the *Journal of the Academy of Safety Researchers* specifically volume 14 winter and ask you to briefly describe for the court the main theme of the article on page 129."

"It's a critique of my paper on the involvement of double bottom trucks in fatal crashes."

"And who is the author of that critique?"

"Eric Cornwell."

"Two years ago were you not a candidate for president of the Academy of Safety Researchers?"

"Yes"

"And who was your opponent?"

"Eric Cornwell."

"Who won?"

"Cornwell."

"Before working for the Safety Research Institute where did you work?"

"I was an Associate Professor and Research Scientist with the HSRC at Midland Sate."

"So you were a colleague of professor Cornwell?"

"Yes"

"Why did you leave HSRC?"

"I got a job at SRI."

"Yes sir, but wasn't there a reason you sought employment elsewhere. Isn't it true that the reason you left HSRC is that you failed to be granted tenure and in essence were fired?"

"I did not get tenure that is true."

"And did not professor Cornwell chair the tenure committee at that time?"

"Yes"

"So let me get this straight in the recent years you lost an election, a contract and a job because of Eric Cornwell. I'd be very angry at a man that cost me so much. You must bear quite a grudge against Eric Cornwell so much so that you would do most anything to get even, maybe even perjury"

"Objection badgering the witness"

"Sustained"

"No further questions."

Carol returned to her position at the prosecution table and looked into the eyes of the jurors. She felt confident that she planted the notion that perhaps Roberts was testifying merely to seek some measure of revenge against a former professional foe. She hoped they would dismiss his criticisms of Cornwell's findings

Goldenbaum's next witnesses testified to Hoag's character and how she was too kind to have committed such a crime. A family friend from the Orlando area recounted how she had taken on a great responsibility in asking to be named guardian of her nephew, and how much she loved him and even paid his tuition at Central Florida. Carol did not want to attack the witnesses. In her assessment what they said was not damaging to her case. After all, nice people sometimes do bad things.

Finally, Goldenbaum rested his case. As Carol had

thought, he did not allow Naomi Hoag to testify. It was now time for closing arguments.

"As I told you in my opening, the State will show you that Naomi Hoag had a motive to kill Jack Victor, the opportunity to kill and the means with which to do it. During the course of this trial we have done this. Jack Victor knew that Ms Hoag did not earn the graduate degree that was a requirement for her position as CEO of Midland General. He threatened to take this information to the Board which would have fired her and damaged her reputation. She could not allow this to happen. So to prevent him, she coerced her nephew into staging an accident that she hoped would result in Jack Victor's death. When he survived the crash she had a second chance to silence him as he lay unconscious in the hospital she ran. As a former nurse she knew how to administer a drug through an IV tube. As CEO she had full rein of the hospital including access to the narcotics cabinet. She was seen in the victim's room moments before his heart stop beating. Sitting here today she may look like a kind hearted grandmother but in truth she is a cold blooded murderer. She had reason to kill Jack Victor and she did. The evidence is clear; you have no other choice but to find her guilty of the crime she is accused of committing."

Now it was Goldenbaum's turn. He stood before the jury box confidently and defiantly and then began his summation.

"Ladies and gentlemen of the Jury. Thank you for exercising your civil duty by giving of your valuable time to sit in that box and listen attentively and to carefully weigh the evidence presented. Soon Judge Hill will give you instructions on your deliberations. Now your job is not to judge the innocence or guilt of Ms. Hoag. No your job is to decide whether or not Ms. Berry presented sufficient evidence to leave no reasonable doubt in your minds that my client is guilty. Let's quickly review that evidence. We all agree that there was a serious crash involving the victim and a Mr. Franklin. Ms. Berry wants you to believe that the crash was not an accident but a deliberate attempt to kill Mr. Victor. Now you have heard two experts in their field disagree on how to determine whether or not the crash was intentional or accidental. After hearing both men, I know I don't have a conclusion that is without some doubt. I know I can not determine which man is correct, I have a lot of doubt and maybe you have some also. You also heard testimony from Mr. Franklin. But who is this Billie Franklin? Well he is the nephew of a loving and caring aunt, but also a drug addict, alcoholic who should be charged with vehicular manslaughter at the least but instead was promised immunity for his testimony. Now is it not at least plausible that if someone is given the opportunity to lie to save himself from a long jail term that he just might lie? Then we come to the testimony of Nurse Perkins. If you hear her carefully all she is really telling you is that my client visited Mr. Victor. Is this not something that someone of compassion would not do? After all Mr. Victor was the chairman of the organization that Ms Hoag works for, in reality her boss. Which one of you would not visit your hospitalized boss, when you are in the same hospital? Are you going to let this simple act of human kindness send a woman to prison? Besides all this shows is that Ms. Hoag visited her friend but not that she had anything to do with an alleged injection. Given all of this, there is grave reasonable doubt. You need to listen to your heart and your mind, the state failed in its attempts to prove beyond a reasonable doubt that my client is guilty of anything. Therefore your only reasonable decision is to acquit my client."

As Goldenbaum concluded he walked to the defense table with a swagger becoming a professional athlete. Carol is less confident. He spoke so eloquently that he almost convinced her as to reasonable doubt.

"Members of the jury. You will now retire to the jury room to deliberate and consider all that you have heard. The court bailiff will be outside your room at all times. Should you need anything or have any questions please ask him."

One by one the jurors left the jury box and entered the small room to begin deliberations. No juror looked at either the defense table or the prosecution table.

"This court is recessed until further notice."

As they left the courtroom Gabriella turned to Carol "Thank you Miss Berry for your efforts. I hope Goldenbaum did not confuse the jury too much."

"You're welcome Mrs. Victor. We never know after summation what the jurors are thinking. All we can do now is wait and hope. The court will call me when the the jury reaches its decision and I will call Mr. Riggs since I have his cell phone number. Get yourself a good meal and some rest. It may be a very long night."

*****

Gary and Gabriella left the courtroom and headed across the street to Arthur's. The popular restaurant was crowded but they decided to wait the estimated twenty minutes for a table. Soon they were seated at a small table next to the window facing the courthouse. Gabriella stared at the old building and thought about what was taking place in a small second floor room. Surely, they would see the logical connection and the link to Hoag and return a guilty verdict. But Goldenbaum did such a masterful job.

Both ordered the evening special; a large porterhouse steak with a baked potato and salad. Gary also ordered a bottle of a Bogle zinfandel. They talked briefly about the trial but mainly remained unusually quiet.

"Oh Gary, I'll be so glad to get this mess over with."

"Me too."

The waiter brought the dinners and they ate and occasionally made small talk. When they both finished the meal the waiter returned.

"Are you finished? Can I take the plate?"

Taking the finished meals the waiter then asked if either cared for dessert.

Gary ordered first, "I think I'll have a cannoli and cup of espresso."

"Me too but a cup of decaf coffee."

As they were finishing the coffees, Gary's cell phone rang

"Hello… yes, so soon… what's this mean? ok we'll be there. That was Carol she just got a call from the court. Apparently the jury has reached a verdict. Judge Hill will reconvene the court at 7:30."

"That's quick they have only been deliberating about two hours, did she give any indication whether or not a quick verdict is good or bad?"

"No she thought it could go either way or maybe they just want to seek more information."

Gabriella and Gary met Carol outside the courtroom.

"Hi guys. I did not expect the jury to reach decision this quickly. I have no idea what to make of the swiftness. They could have already reached a verdict or they may want the court to reconvene so they can review the evidences or ask for a clarification. I don't know. Well let's go in and see."

Shortly after, the jury again walked one by one and took their respective seats in the jury box. Each one wore a somber look, and again made no eye contact with either defense or prosecution.

"Has the jury reached a verdict?"

"Yes we have your honor."

The forelady then handed the bailiff a folded slip of paper that he gave to the Judge. Judge Hill read the paper and gave it back to the bailiff.

"Madam forelady how say you?"

"In the matter of the state versus Naomi Hoag we the jury find the defendant Naomi Hoag... guilty of all charges."

Judge Hill then asked each member whether that was his or her decision and each responded yes.

"Ladies and gentlemen of the jury, having reached a unanimous decision in this matter you are hereby dismissed with the appreciation and gratitude of the court. Ms. Hoag you have been found guilty of all charges by a jury of peers. You are hereby sentenced to remain in the county jail pending a sentencing hearing to be held in this location two months from today. This court is adjourned."

After hearing the verdict Gabriella sat motionless for awhile as if in a state of stupor. After a few moments she got up and gave Carol a big hug and then kissed Gary tenderly.

"Carol, Thank you so much for your hard work. I know Jack is somewhere watching with a big smile of appreciation on his face."

By now the courtroom is almost empty. The attorneys were putting their papers and notes into their attaché cases. Goldenbaum approached the prosecution table with less cockiness and swagger but still with a bit of arrogance. He held out his hand in a congratulatory fashion.

"Congratulations counselor, nicely done. If you ever decide to make some real money and defend the bad guys give me a call. We can always use a cute and bright skirt in the office." He winked and gestured with his index finger and thumb

"Hasta la vista;" he exited the courtroom as arrogant as ever.

Carol stood there silent for a moment then shook her head and laughed. She thought "this skirt's gonna get a beer."

She left the courtroom and went out the Walnut Street entrance and met the gathered horde of reporters. As she stood on the steps answering questions, Gary and Gabriella left by the parking garage, quietly got into the car and headed south toward Lake Road.

As Gary turned onto Lake Road, Gabriella felt herself at ease for the first time in little over a year. Her heart did not ache nor her legs tense as the car passed the fatal ravine. She thought that now she was ready to get on with the rest of her life. Naomi Hoag was found guilty and Jack's good reputation remained untarnished. Justice had been served.

*****

As Gary parked the car in the driveway and they walked up the pathway to the front door he took Gabriella's hand. They stood on the stoop facing each other. He could no longer keep silent what he held in his heart this past year.

"Gabby, now that the trial and everything is over I got to tell you what I wanted to say for a long long time. I kept silent for fear of offending you but I think or hope that you know how much..." Gabriella gently put her index finger on his lips-

"Ssh" with that she gently kissed him. As their lips parted their eyes remained fixed upon each other. She pulled his body close to hers, put her arms around him and they kissed passionately. She put the house keys into his right hand and said "Carpe Diem".

He opened the door and the two ascended the stairs.

The End

Printed in the United States
132201LV00001B/7/P